SINGAPORE PASSAGE

This is the story of a race from Singapore
to Canton between two barks, *The Forest
of Arden* and *The Firefly*. Both ships carry
cargoes of the finest opium and the first
there will make the best prices. On board
the *Arden* are two women, Anne Mackenzie,
the daughter of Sir Gordon Mackenzie, who
is bound for Canton; and Shen Ti, who was
press-ganged from an opium den. Only
after sailing was it discovered that she was a
girl.

Abner, the *Arden's* skipper, puts into the
Paracel Islands to carry out repairs sustained
during a battle with the *Firefly*. Here they
run into trouble from threatening natives
and from mutiny. But with Anne's help
Abner gets the *Arden* away, makes a deal
with a native ruffian and is able to head for
Macao—and happiness.

A rousing tale of the South China Seas in
the days of sail, spiced with piracy, mutiny,
treachery and tough fighting, through which
also runs the thread of high romance.

SINGAPORE PASSAGE

By

DONALD BARR CHIDSEY

Author of " Elizabeth I ", etc.

WILDSIDE PRESS

First published in Great Britain 1957

Chapter One

THE SMOKE, a yellowish-blue in colour, hung in languid ribbons. When it was stirred at all—not often, for this was a quiet place—it moved lumpily, limp at the ends. It had a thick, sweet smell, a smell that could turn your stomach if you were not used to it.

Every bunk was occupied. Most of the pipers lay still, perhaps smiling at the ceiling or chanting a little inner song to themselves so that their lips moved without a sound. They were feeble fellows, fuzzy at the edges. A stranger from the Occident might have called them fiends; but they looked harmless enough, and even slightly comic.

One, moving as though in a dream—and indeed he was—sat up. There was a lamp and a ball of black, viscid stuff wrapped in dried leaves on the taboret at his elbow. He pried some of this stuff loose with a small stick, around which he wrapped it, turning and turning it to keep the stuff from falling off. He held it over the flame of the lamp for a moment. It spluttered, hissing. The man popped it into the bowl of his pipe, inhaled twice at great length, and then leaned back against a bare wall, grinning as though pleased with himself, trying to hold the smoke in. This was not good opium, for it had been cooked and cooked again, the scrapings of pipes often rescraped; but it was the best such a coolie could afford, and he strove to make it go far.

The proprietor watched him, not moving, or even blinking. The proprietor himself, hunkered down on his heels, didn't indulge. Somebody, he must have reasoned, had to stay sane around that den.

There was a knock on the door. The proprietor stiffened. This was late, past midnight. All his regulars had reported, in addition to a few others, among them a couple of Lascar seamen, who lay now in poppied slumber, each mouth a smirk. There was no light outside. No more customers could be expected. On the other hand, at least two ships were to sail to-night; and this caller might seek recruits. Captains and mates, the proprietor knew, sometimes had forceful ways of refilling their forecastles. Nor could he sound any sort of alarm. In this particular alley near the Dragon's Teeth Gate, Singapore, in the year of Our Lord 1835, if you went out after nightfall you walked warily, and you damn well minded your own business.

The knocking was repeated. It was loud, peremptory.

The proprietor snicked a long, thin, exceedingly bright knife out of his left sleeve and studied this for a moment. He replaced it. He rose and shuffled to the door.

When he opened this it was with the greatest circumspection. The slit was less than an inch across. No foot could have been inserted.

His fears were confirmed. Here was a white man, tall, glowering.

" Any of my hands here, Funnyface? "

The proprietor started to close the door.

Something streaked through the opening, something shiny, metallic. The proprietor's hand on the latch was seized from above and below by a claw-like device, a pair of extension pliers, so that he squealed at the pain that shot along his arm like fire.

"A little invention of my own," the visitor said. "Smart, eh? I call it the Persuader. Now step aside, Funnyface. I'm coming in."

When Abner Smith, first mate of the *Forest of Arden*, did enter the den it was neither swiftly nor slowly. He did not swagger. Nor would he fumble; for thoroughness was a fixed habit of his. He had a job to do and he was serious about it.

He carried a sheath knife, and his hands, though large, were limber and could quickly become fists. He put away the "persuader", but he was careful not to turn his back upon the proprietor; in fact he brushed him ahead, sweeping him forward bit by bit with his glance. The proprietor did not resist. He knew better.

In the middle of the room Abner paused. He did not gawp, didn't rubber his neck; for though he was only twenty-three this was his fourth trip out East, and the sight of an opium den was nothing new. However, he did swivel his eyes. He nodded.

"That one," at the first Lascar, "and that one," at the other. "How many pipes have they had?"

The proprietor all but purred, and inside his sleeve he relaxed his grip on the knife. The average ship's officer, at least late at night like this, would not have offered to pay.

"Six each," he said eagerly.

"You're a liar. They've only been ashore an hour and a half, and before that they hadn't had a pull since Calcutta, more'n a month back. They couldn't have stayed awake for six pipes—even of your muck. I'll pay for six altogether. Three each. Here."

The proprietor made no objection. Why should he? Already, as a matter of primary precaution, he had picked the Lascars' pockets.

"Lift one," commanded Abner. "You first."

He waited until the proprietor was half-way to the door before hoisting the other Lascar. He wasn't going to get caught with his arms full.

Some of the men in the bunks slept. Others, propped on elbows, beaming fatuously, watched the departure.

It was good to be out in the air again, muggy as that air was, not a bit like the air of Stonington, Connecticut. Abner Smith inhaled gratefully.

The proprietor dumped his load, then scuttled away like a crab. Abner dumped him. They might have been handling sacks of flour.

That made seven sailors, all Asiatic, on the low, wooden-wheeled dray that took up so much of this mean little alley. None stirred. They were all stupefied, sent to sticky slumber by the black stuff in the pipes.

Another Stonington boy, Paul " Pooch " Palmer, scarcely seventeen but a sailor since shaverhood, came out of the place next door, a brothel. He was the third mate, and it was his first trip East.

"Not a one."

Abner shook his head. He did not curse, for he was not a blasphemous man; he did not, however, feel in the best of spirits.

"We got to get one more. And yet if we don't catch that tide at four bells we're stuck here another day, and *Firefly*'ll beat us."

The two Yankee vessels—*Firefly* was a brig, out of Boston—were carrying the same cargo to the same port, Canton. At this season of the north-east monsoon few ships risked that run, and therefore the first of these two to arrive would command by far the best price for what it had to sell. A great deal was at stake. It might amount to a quarter of a million dollars. Neither Ab nor his friend Pooch would share directly in this, even if *Forest of Arden* won the race. With them it was in part a matter of pride but in part, too, a virulent dislike of *Firefly*'s skipper, the tough, truculent MacHarg, who in various far-flung ports of the world had given them ample cause for this feeling. Abner Smith also dreamed of having his own command. If the present voyage was successful financially, that dream might well come true.

A voice spoke behind him: "We'll catch the tide, mister, if you get those hands like I told you to."

Andrew Thompson was a hard man. Heavy-set, block-like of build, he looked stupid—but he wasn't. He was a shrewd dealer; and if he got his bargains not by whispering in corners but rather by thumping the table, nevertheless he did get them. There were some skippers who were all smiles ashore, when raising a crew or a cargo, but fiends off soundings; and these, likely as not, when they made a port put on their "land manners" precisely as they put on their best shirts, preparing to smile again. This was not so of Andy Thompson, who was no hypocrite; he was as vicious ashore as he was afloat.

"I'm going to Laurey's," Thompson said. "Call for me there in a little while, as soon as you get these carcasses below deck. Never mind about looking up that passenger—Mackenzie. If he ain't aboard, too bad. I ain't seen him yet, but I got his fare from his agent." The skipper looked at Third Mate Palmer. " Guess you'll have to bunk up with him."

" Yes," Palmer said miserably.

" Well, let's see what we got here——"

It was dark in the alley, and the captain had to lean over, squinting, in order to examine the prostrate sailors. Of course he would check them, no matter who they were, no matter what the hour, the circumstances, the price or the conditions. For all his rages and the violence of his punishments, Captain Thompson never let a figure slip. He never misplaced a decimal point. He would take everything that wasn't tied down.

" There's only seven! Damn it, Smith, I told you to get eight! "

" These were all we could find, sir. And we've been everywhere. The others must've had friends here. They must've slipped across to Johore. I hear tell the sultan there is taking anything comes along."

" God damn it, what do you care whether they're our men or not? Grab anything! Here——"

The owner of the establishment from which Abner had just extracted the two Lascars was back at his doorway. With the speed of a cat, and an agility altogether astonishing in so large a man, Captain Thompson sprang there in time to get a foot in. The proprietor, himself a big man, tried to shove him away. But Thompson wasn't to be shoved. Bellowing like a bull, he threw himself full-force against the door, so that the proprietor was sent spinning down his own hallway, while the door itself was slammed back against the wall.

" Come on, Smith. We haven't got all night."

Unhappy, though impassive, Abner followed him. Kidnapping—only they didn't call it that: they called it shanghaiing—was an accepted practice in the ports. Abner Smith did not like it. In the first place, it was an admission either of a lack of foresightedness, or else, as in this case, that you served an unpopular skipper; and either of these was bad for business and a man's reputation. In the second place, you got the dregs, the very worst of the drunks and dopes and beaten-up bums. In the third place, it happened to be against the law.

But—the captain had spoken. Abner was only first mate. Orders were orders. He went.

Thompson paused at the entrance to the bunk room, and his nose wrinkled up at the stink.

"Take any one," he commanded. He pointed to the nearest bunk, where there was a nondescript and no doubt unconscious bundle of rags. "Here—take him."

The proprietor broke into shrill protest. "*No—not that one!*"

"Shut up," said Andy Thompson, and started to go out.

He had turned his back on the proprietor, something Abner Smith would never have done. It was incredible that anybody would attach so much importance to one miserable—and not even very large—smoker. True, the bundle of rags might have neglected to pay his chit; but that scarcely justified drawing a knife against Andrew Thompson.

Abner saw the knife. He was on his way to the nearest bunk and was slightly behind the proprietor though watching him, when from a corner of his eye he caught the quick movement. He stepped sideways, reaching out. He caught the man's right arm at the wrist and twisted it swiftly behind his back. The man squealed in pain. Andy Thompson turned, cursing. He took in the situation and reacted in characteristic fashion. Abner already as good as had the knife. The proprietor's right arm was pinioned behind him. Captain Thompson punched the man full in the face.

It was a cruel blow. Thompson was powerful, and he'd swung with all his weight and strength. It might well have smashed the man's jaw.

The proprietor was yanked out of Abner's grip as though by a hurricane. Whirling like a dervish, he reeled across the room, struck a taboret, knocking the lamp off it, and collapsed against the far wall.

The lamp's chimney tinkled to bits. The wick touched some of the matting that skimpily covered the floor. The resulting flame was a stodgy one, for there wasn't enough real air in this room to support a proper fire.

"And be quick about it," called Captain Thompson over his shoulder.

Abner hoisted the sleeper from the nearest bunk. The man certainly was no Hercules and he felt soft as well. But Abner had his orders; he didn't have time to go around feeling muscles. With the inert form slung limply over his left shoulder, Abner straightened the lamp, stamped out the fire, put the taboret back into place.

The smoke swirled and somebody giggled; but even the pipers who still had their eyes open did not seem to see anything. The man who was singing went on and on, tunelessly, monotonously.

Abner paused a moment before the proprietor, who sat with his back against a wall, his legs showing lifeless before him like those of some calico doll. His eyes were glassy. Blood was beginning to come out of both corners of his mouth.

Abner fetched a small sigh, and shook his head. A certain amount of slamming around was all very well, and no doubt it was needed, but he was sick of Andy Thompson's insensate, unceasing savagery. He wished he could straighten the place up before he left. He wished he could bring the proprietor back to his senses.

"*Smith!* Where the hell are you?"

"Coming, sir."

Chapter Two

SINGAPORE WAS silent; and as they pushed the dray along streets, through air so thick and wet as to be almost like water itself, they might have been gnomes from some nether region who in sombre glee trundled souls to oblivion. Sometimes the wheels squealed as though in protest, a sound fit to set your nerves on edge. Sometimes a figure stirred, blubbering; but for the most part they lay still. The houses and shops, their windows boarded against the night, loomed in glum menace on either side, leaning (or so it seemed) a little towards them. And all the while they trailed the sickish odour of opium.

Abner and Pooch said nothing. They had no need to; and neither was a chatty person. Nor did Kok Soo speak, at the foot of the gangplank, when he surveyed the dray-load. Instead, the bos'n, a marvellously efficient man, merely whistled for his two tindals, Chinese like himself, and the three of them pitched in to unload, carrying the hands, one by one, forward to the forecastle. It was not the first time that they had done this. It was, traditionally, part of a bos'n's job.

Pooch and Abner brushed themselves off and lit cigars.

"Everything a-tauto?" Ab asked the bos'n.

Kok Soo nodded. Whether because of natural taciturnity or because of self-consciousness about his English, or both, this squat, imperturbable powerful *serang*, or bos'n, seldom did open his mouth.

"That passenger aboard? That missionary—Mackenzie?"

Kok Soo rolled his eyes, swallowing, and an odd expression came to his face, where there seldom was any expression at all. For a moment he looked as though about to speak, but he only nodded.

"There's one for you, Pooch," Abner said carelessly. "Want to meet your new cabin mate now, or will you wait?"

"I reckon I can wait."

The bark *Forest of Arden* was not a large one, and the after quarters, the officers' quarters, were almost as jam-packed as the forecastle—two tiny cabins, each with two bunks, and the corridor between them was so narrow that you had to turn sideways if you passed anybody in it. Since sailors are out of all humanity the men most inured to discomfort, ordinarily these quarters would have given no cause for complaint. But to share them with a lime-juicer, a psalm-singer, an L.M.S. send-out for Canton in a ridiculous effort to convert the heathen Chinee—and to endure this for weeks on end, all the while beating up against the north-east monsoon, fighting for every inch of way—this was no pretty prospect. It was Pooch Palmer who'd get the worst of it. He would have to share a cabin with this A. Mackenzie, whom neither of them as yet had met. A passenger had been accepted only because the second mate was down with fever here in Singapore, where it had proved impossible to sign on another officer in time to race the *Firefly* to Canton. This made it hard on the third mate, Pooch, who in addition was going to have to stand extra watches because of the absence of the second; but clearly there would be no sense in sailing with an empty bunk when somebody was willing to pay for it. Abner, of course, bunked in with the skipper.

Now Pooch made a face and drew on his cigar to help rid his head of the cloying fumes of opium.

"I guess I can stand it," he said.

Abner, puffing his own cigar, studied the lad sideways. Yes, he reckoned that Pooch could stand it. Abner should know. How many times, as boys, they had fought side by side. There was always some fighting going on in those days, as Abner remembered them. The boys from the nearest town, Westerly, used to come to Stonington looking for trouble. Or else a group of Stonington boys would go to Westerly with the same purpose in mind. It seemed it had always been like that, and always would be. Nobody knew what had started it. It was an institution, that feud, a semi-permanent war. The Westerly lads called themselves Buckies, the Stonington lads were Fishtails, and they had some spirited to-dos.

It was in the midst of such a fracas that Abner Smith first noticed Palmer, still so young he should never have been allowed to come along. Pooch had been down, and a couple of Buckies had been booting him about the head when Abner interrupted. Later, Abner had helped the dazed, bleeding boy back home, where he met, for the first time, Pooch's widowed mother. Mrs. Theodosia Palmer had been kind to Ab; and not many people were being kind to the Smith boy, an orphan, in those days. She was the nearest thing to a mother that Abner had ever known, and though he did not say anything about it, he guessed he pretty well worshipped Mrs. Palmer. Certainly he made it a point to squire Mrs. Palmer's belligerent son Pooch. He might have saved himself the trouble. This particular Fishtail, small though he was then, had needed no bodyguard. "You must've been born swinging your fists," folks would say. "You'd have to ask Mother about that," Pooch would reply.

And now here he was, at seventeen, clear around to the other side of the world, the pugilistic Pooch, quiet, embarrassed, awkward, strong, faithful. Here he was, third mate of a bark moored to Collyer Quay, a monstrous great distance from Stonington; and in the eyes of Ab Smith he was still a small boy, made to look smaller indeed by the incongruous cigar he smoked, by the exotic surroundings in which he stood. But he could take care of himself. Ab did not worry about that.

"Yes," Ab said after a while, "I guess you can stand it."

From the quay, from the foot of the gangway, Abner regarded the *Arden*'s rig. Aye, she was ready. Twenty minutes after he had fetched the skipper they would be moving towards the outer roads, towards the open sea. He was sure of it.

The bark's artillery, scant enough at best, was properly

in place, Abner also noted. In addition to a lockerful of rifles and other small arms, she carried two thick black carronades amidships, on deck, one on each side, for which ports had been cut into the gunnel, and astern, on the poop, a large pivot-gun. The waters northwards to Canton swarmed with pirates, and many a vessel never got through, never was seen again.

Abner nodded, pleased.

Well, he was not worried about the bark itself or its rigs; these were in the best possible shape. Nor was he worried about the cargo, stowed under his own supervision. He *was* worried about the human element, the crew. There would be only three officers now, instead of four, since the second mate, West, would stay in Singapore with his fever. Kok Soo and his assistants were excellent workers; but after all, they were Chinese, and Ab never would be able to understand them. The captain's striker, Yok, was a Tamil and virtually half-witted. The Lord only knew— and perhaps the Lord cared—what that man they had just shanghaied was; but whatever he was, he'd have an ugly temper when he came to.

The Lascars would be even worse, and there were still seventeen of them, after desertions. They had endured Captain Thompson and his echo, West, on the whole hot run from Calcutta. They had taken their beatings, their kickings, their canings—West carried a whippy rattan, which he used on all possible occasions, bringing it across the tenderest spots—until they had almost reached a point of rebellion. They were meek men, on the whole, but they had their limits. They hated Andy Thompson, understandably, as they hated West. They also hated Pooch Palmer and First Mate Smith. Pooch and Abner had

B

only been carrying out orders, but these had been Andy Thompson's orders.

Secretly both Ab and Pooch had felt sorry for the hands, and had done what they could to alleviate their lot; but their efforts had gone unnoticed, and the first mate, like the third, had been and would be hated by the men. Never turn your back! Abner all but shuddered when he wondered what would happen after the doped hands had recovered their wits, far out at sea. He hoped that the weather held, though it probably wouldn't. They were starting this run at the worst possible time of the year.

He preferred not to think about it, and turned to Kok Soo and said, " I go captain."

" Allee-samee catchum-up," added Pooch Palmer, who liked to practise his pidgin.

Once again the bos'n looked to be on the point of saying something, but once again he shut his mouth and lowered his head as he turned away.

And Abner Smith, his thumbs hooked into the top of his breeches, started up South Bridge Street.

The place called Laurey's, as much an agent's office as a bar, was the unofficial headquarters of many of the passing-through skippers. Not infrequently, last-minute deals were completed there, last minute details attended to. No place in the city of Singapore was safe after dark; but Laurey's, comparatively speaking, was almost respectable. As Ab approached it he was thinking only of shipboard duties, as a first mate should, though he did wonder from time to time when he would get a command of his own.

The first hint he had that anything was wrong came in the form of a sibilant whisper from one of the windows. These windows were shuttered against marauders, but the cracks were large, and it would appear that Abner had been seen. There was a scuffling, quickly ended. Then the light was whuffed out.

Ab came to a stop, scratching his chin with a thumbnail. There was no sound. He shook his head. He went up to the door and tried it. It was locked, bolted with a balk. He hammered it.

"Open up here! I've come for Captain Thompson! Open it up!"

Silence.

"I'm going to get Andy Thompson," Abner shouted. "Either you open this door or I'll smash it in. I'll count three. *One——*"

He tightened his belt, hunched up his shoulders.

"*Two——*"

The door was thrown open. Captain Thompson came hurtling out.

"Here's your god-damn skipper," somebody cried.

The door was slammed shut again, the bolt thrown home.

Andrew Thompson sprawled on his back. When Abner knelt beside him he easily found the knife, which indeed fell free of its own accord.

"Get me away from here!" the skipper whispered. "Get me to Ah Sim's! Before they come out and finish the job!"

Twenty minutes later, pale, still dizzy, and pitifully weak from loss of blood, but as grim and as poisonous as ever, he glared up from a bed.

"I know who the son of a whore was that did it," he confided, "and I'll get him if I have to stay in this hole all summer. But I'm no good now. Take her out, anyway.

You've *got* to beat the *Firefly*. Here's your first command, mister, and by God, if you don't make a go of it——"

A fit of coughing stopped him.

A moment later: "All right, get out. Ah Sim can take care of me. Now get the hell out of here."

Chapter Three

THE OFFICERS, who'd had little enough sleep the night before, would get no sleep at all the first night out. There was God's plenty to do—the tug to pay for, last-minute fresh-fruit supplies to be stored, the final papers to sign and final port fees to pay, the pilot to be put overside. There were cables to cast off, lines to be reeved, look-outs to be posted, soundings made. There was the canvas to be cracked on, and then, once they were outside, in the open sea, re-spread. There were a thousand other things to keep him and Pooch on deck. The sky was streaked with dawn, while the dark green coast of Malaya was well astern, before either of them even so much as got a chance to go on to the head.

The bark *Forest of Arden*, built at Saybrook, Connecticut, only a few years before, was rated at three hundred and fifty tons. She looked even smaller. Though she was not roomy, and though just now her bottom might have done with a scraping, what with her clippered hull and extremely tall sticks she was fast. But she was a roller! Given any kind of sea—and they were likely to be given all kinds, more or less at once, on a run like this—she would take a tremendous amount of green water aboard. Her forecastle surely and sometimes the cabins as well might be wet for days and even weeks together. You had to pay for such speed. You didn't get it for nothing.

As the dawn came, opening up the sea, Ab Smith scanned it anxiously. He saw one sampan and a smattering of native proas; nothing else; no sign of the *Firefly*.

Forward and aft alike, the *Forest* was short-handed. The officer contingent had been cut in half. And most of what men she did have in her forecastle were motionless there in poppied slumber. An opium jag takes a long time to sleep off.

Yet all the responsibility for getting this vessel over twelve hundred miles of uncharted seas, past reefs and pirate islands, all in the teeth of the notorious north-east monsoon at the worst possible season of the year—rested upon Abner Smith.

He was a skipper, sure enough. Well, the joy could come later. Right now he had too much to do. He couldn't take the time to exult.

It was three bells, and fully light, when at last he sent a staggering Pooch Palmer below.

"You need it more'n I do. Besides, you're itching to find out what your cabin mate looks like. Funny he hasn't showed up yet. Must be a late sleeper. Or else sick."

It was not until then, when at last he had the poop to himself—for everything was spread and he had sent the helmsman forward to get his own relief, taking over the wheel—that Abner drew an enormous breath and shut his eyes for an instant and thought of himself as Captain Smith.

His head ached, his eyes throbbed, his mouth was dry. He was hungry, and so tired that he had to cling to the wheel for support. He hadn't had a wink of sleep in thirty-odd hours. Yet—he had never felt better.

Captain!

He lifted his head and beamed like a lunatic at the flagrantly opalescent sky.

Captain!

"Er—Abner——"

His mate, his one officer, Paul Palmer of Stonington, stood swaying at the head of the cabin ladder. Pooch's eyes were tennis balls. His face was as white as a manifest.

"What's come over you, mister? A. Mackenzie keeping you awake singing hymns, is he? Whyn't you slap him on the snout?"

"Ab—he's—it's—this Mackenzie——"

"What in thunderation's the matter, man?"

"Mackenzie is a—*woman*!"

From below him, from the foot of the ladder, came a clear melodious voice: "May I come up? I'm Anne Mackenzie. It looks like a perfectly lovely day, and I do want to meet the captain."

Chapter Four

S H E W E N T with the morning, complementing it. Trim, she moved with ease, and showed no trace of the landsman's usual clumsiness.

A small woman, adroitly curved, she might have been twenty, nothing but a girl. She had a fine smile, for she seemed sincerely glad to be alive, and glad to be meeting Abner Smith. She had a roundish face, large round brown eyes, a remarkably small mouth, small chin, and the faintest conceivable splash of freckles across her small but strong nose. So very faint were these freckles that she might easily have concealed them with powder, but her face showed no powder, and except in this one respect needed none. Her eyes laughed up at Abner. She had a deep dimple high on each cheek.

"You are Captain Thompson, I take it?"

"Acting Captain Smith, ma'am," corrected Abner, as he took his cap off. "Captain Thompson met with a—a slight accident."

"Oh, I hope he's not badly hurt?"

"They expect him to recover, ma'am."

It was a wonder of wonders how she had managed to get herself all togged out, all neat and clean like this, in a cabin so tiny and so low that even she might have had difficulty standing upright there. Yet she didn't stew and fuss. The moment she raised her head above deck level the wind took her hair and began to flip wisps of it here and there, but she paid it no mind. The hair was a rich brown, matching the eyes, and there were flecks of red in it. It was wavy and thick, and not long.

The deck might have been pneumatic, the way she stood. Abner could not see her feet, but he had the feeling, almost, that she was balanced on her toes like a dancer, vibrant, tense, and expectant.

Even the dress she wore—blue-grey turned over with white, plain, well-starched, but by no means puritanical—

seemed to have a life of its own. She filled it exquisitely. Just as some women can't linger in a strong light, so others should never venture to stand in a strong wind. But this woman could.

Abner realized with a start that he was embarrassing her with his gawping stare.

"At your service, ma'am," he mumbled.

She laughed. "Forgive me, captain, but you look so—so startled. Of course you expected me to be a man?"

"Well, I did."

"You wouldn't have taken me as a passenger if you'd known I was female? And neither would Captain Thompson?"

"Well, no. Nothing personal, of course."

"Of course not." She took to frowning at the horizon as if it were a long word the spelling of which she wished to memorize. "Everywhere I've come out this way, I've found that same feeling. Why? What's the matter with us women?"

"Why, they're all right, I reckon. Mighty nice sex, in lots of ways. But not on shipboard. Ships just weren't built with women in mind. That ain't my fault, ma'am. But—maybe I'd better put back."

"Nonsense!"

He looked directly at her, and it was an easy thing to do. She glowered at that horizon now, as though it had just played her a dirty trick.

"Why is it nonsense, ma'am?"

"Because if you put back now it'll cost you at least two days, and then you'll never beat the *Firefly* to Canton. Which will mean a small fortune to your owners. Oh, I

know something about your business, captain! I learned
it from your agent in Singapore, Mr. Cunningham."

"Still and all, if I decide——"

"And it would cost you more than that, captain! It
would change all my plans and keep me penned up for
weeks in Malaya, maybe even for months. So of course
I'd sue the ship."

"Ma'am, I would see to it that your fare was returned
in full."

"It isn't the fare I'm talking about. Of course I'd get
that back. But I'd sue you for breach of contract. Because
when I bought this passage, captain, I as good as signed a
contract, and so did your agent at the same time. In the
eyes of the law it was just as if it had been written out and
signed and sealed and witnessed and stamped and regis-
tered. And if you don't know that, you should—a man in
your position."

He swallowed. "Ma'am, if——"

"How could anybody possibly have a stronger case, I'd
like to know? Why, I'd be awarded thousands. And I'd
make a fool of you at the same time."

"Ma'am, you can't say that——"

"Do you, by chance, captain, have any awareness of
how much her Gracious Majesty's servants in the Straits
Settlements abominate Yankee traders?"

"But when deception's been practised——"

"There was no deception of any sort. I bought this
passage as A. Mackenzie, and A. Mackenzie I am and
always have been. My first name is Anne, in case you're
interested. I wore no disguise and I told no lies."

"Ma'am, all I said was——"

"Can I help it if the officers of this vessel aren't con-

cerned enough with a passenger to take a look at her first?
I wasn't smuggled in rolled up in a rug, like Cleopatra.
I *walked* aboard. And did I meet a single white man here?
No. It was a Chinese who showed me down to my cabin.
Very courteous fellow, too."

So that was why Kok Soo acted so strange when asked
about the passenger, was Ab's first thought. He'd have a
few words with him later.

What he said aloud was: "I always did think that
Cunningham was crooked. Now I know. He never
would have sold you that passage—you, a woman—unless
you'd greased him good."

"You'd have an easy time proving *that* in court, now
wouldn't you, captain?"

She was absolutely right, and he stared at her in amazement.

Abner Smith had never had anything to do with
missionaries. He didn't know what he had expected them
to be like. But certainly not like this! No female, dedi-
cated or otherwise, had any right to have brains and grit
both.

"If you know so much about shipping in these parts,"
he said, "why didn't you buy passage aboard the *Firefly*?"

"I tried to. They wouldn't take me."

"I see. Their agent wasn't to be bribed, eh?"

She made no reply to this.

"A pity," Ab went on, "because they're said to be a
very fast vessel. They got the start on us because we had
some trouble collecting our hands. And we may never
overhaul them."

"Oh, I wouldn't say that, captain." Suddenly her tone
was light. "If you were to crack on stunsails——"

"Eh?"

"That may not be the *Firefly*, about two points off the starboard bow, captain," and she pointed, "but it certainly is a sail of some sort."

Ab snatched the glass from its leather case beside the binnacle and sprang for the foremast shrouds. Within ten seconds he was dropping into the crow's nest and kicking the look-out awake.

The vessel was far ahead and, as that astounding woman had said, a couple of points to starboard. She could be the *Firefly*, probably was. She was hull down, indeed not always visible, but he believed he recognized her rig.

She was on the starboard tack just then, and he studied her for a long time, trying to make out her course. She was much farther east than he had expected her to be, if ever he picked her up. And she had more eastering on her right now, he calculated, than the *Forest of Arden* had. That would take her perilously close to the Paracels, a tangle of reefs and nigger-heads and coral mushrooms, with a few gritty beaches, that ran a hundred-odd miles north and south, notorious even as nautical graveyards in the South China Sea went.

Abner had laid his own course close to the Paracels, meaning to save mileage. Now he decided to lay it even closer.

He descended to the deck. Anne Mackenzie greeted him with a warm smile. There was nothing triumphant about that smile. She seemed genuinely glad to see him again.

"You've decided not to put about, I take it?"

"Aye."

He gave the helmsman the new course, north-by-north-east-a-point-north, admonishing him to steer small.

Anne Mackenzie was still smiling. She held out her hand.

"We shouldn't start this way, captain. It's going to prove a long hard pull, from all I hear, and there's no profit in us making it worse, is there?"

"Ma'am," he said, "that's sense."

He took the hand. It was firm, and it was warm.

"It's only fair that you know what I am doing here, really. I didn't lie to you, captain. But maybe I didn't quite tell all the truth. Would you like to hear the rest?"

"Ma'am," he said, "I sure would."

"I won't apologize," she began, "because I don't think I have anything to apologize for. But I promise to stay out of your way as much as possible. I haven't had anythink like your experience at sea, naturally. Still this is my fourth ship, so I'm not entirely a lubber. After all, I've hardly set foot on land in the past four months."

"It's a long haul from London," Ab conceded.

"I won't get sick. I never do. And if you can't expect me to climb the ratlines the way you did a little while ago, or help to walk the hook up, or holystone the deck—well, anyway, at least I can keep my own cabin clean."

This reminded Ab of his mate, who had been standing by, too embarrassed to take any part in the conversation. Pooch sagged, understandably; but for all his weariness he stood spellbound, his mouth an O. Abner brought him to attention with a nod.

"Better transfer your gear to my cabin, mister. I'll have you topside again at eight bells. That's all."

"Aye, aye, sir."

"Sleep well, Mr. Palmer," said Anne Mackenzie.

"Thank you, ma'am."

For some time after Pooch had gone the skipper and his passenger, forearms on the rail, stared at the sail that probably belonged to the *Firefly*.

"One thing I can do," she said suddenly. "One thing I'm good at."

"What's that?"

"Figures. Do you keep accounts on this ship? You must. I can handle any kind of ledger and make it come out right. I was my uncle's secretary for more than two years. Not at his office, of course. At his home. But I handled all his accounts. He's an importer."

Non-committal, Ab Smith nodded. In all truth, the *Forest*'s books were something he looked forward to examining, for Andy Thompson had been close with them and Ab knew little of the financial affairs of the ship, a limited liability company in itself, a floating corporation. Abner did know, though, that seamanship was only half of a captain's qualifications for his post—and maybe not the more important half either. His ability to drive a bargain, to keep accounts, to report a profit: this counted more with the men at home, the money men, than his popularity with the crew or even the condition in which he brought his vessel back. And it was in this field that Ab was weak, since he'd never had any money, or the control of any money.

However, book-keeping, right now, was the last thing he was interested in. He shook an impatient head.

"I'm sorry I was rude back there."

"You weren't at all, captain."

"But I still can't understand it. I can't understand how

the London Missionary Society could be so stupid as to send you 'way out here."

" I beg your pardon? "

" Nothing personal. I mean send a woman out here. They ought to know better. Why, ma'am, you couldn't even get *into* China, not even if you was a man, much less set up any kind of a mission there. Nearest you can come is Macao, which is an island."

" But the factories———"

" They're up at Jackass Point, but still outside the walls of Canton, ma'am. You can't even get up there unless you're a man and have an officially approved business connection with the Russells or the Dents of Jardine-Matheson or some other big firm. And even then you can't move outside of the compound."

" Perhaps the rules will be relaxed? "

" More likely to be made stricter."

She nodded, then smiled up at Abner Smith.

" Very well," she said, " then I'll go to Macao and see what I can do with the servants and such, and wait for my chance. That's the way Arthur would have done it, if he'd lived."

" Who was Arthur? "

" A missionary."

" But then—what are you? "

" His sister. And survivor. He died in the Cape Colony, that Dutch place at the southern tip of Africa. He's buried at the foot of Table Mountain. He was a really fine man, captain."

" Maybe," suggested Ab, " you'd better start at the beginning."

" You're right. Well, then, my brother and I were

orphans, and he was a minister of the Church, and he heard a call to carry the Word of God to the benighted Chinese. It's as simple as that."

"I see nothing simple about it at all."

"Well, he went to the London Missionary Society people and asked them to send him out East. It meant everything in the world to him. But the L.M.S. people were afraid to risk it. They'd heard that China was closed to everybody except a very few licensed traders."

"They heard right."

"They refused to finance him. So he said he'd finance himself, though he had no funds of his own, nothing. And he went to my uncle, whose private secretary I was— as I told you before—and asked him to back the trip. My uncle's a rich man, captain. Gordon Mackenzie of the firm of Mackenzie and Blair. You may have heard of him?"

Abner's jaw dropped as abruptly as though somebody had pulled a coupling pin out of it. Why, Sir Gordon Mackenzie was more than a mere trader—he was a merchant prince. He must be one of the wealthiest men in England.

"I didn't want Arthur to go," the girl went on. "His health was poor and I didn't think he could stand the voyage. But he was bound and determined to. So I said that if he went I'd go with him, to take care of him. Uncle Gordon approved of that arrangement. In fact he said he wouldn't pay for the passage unless it was done that way— both of us going."

"But then he'd lose you as his private secretary."

"In a way, yes. But I'd still be working for him. You see, Uncle Gordon had been thinking for a long while of branching out. He'd been considering the Far East. He has considerable money that he needs to put to work. He isn't afraid of bucking the John Company "—she meant the Honourable East India Company— "but he doesn't know much about China. And it's hard to learn, in England, captain. Men who go out to China stay there for five, six, seven years or more, and when they come back they're not the same men who went away. For one thing, they're ridiculously loyal to their firms, even though they've retired. As far as I can make out, being a trader in China is something like belonging to a very exclusive club."

Abner Smith gave her one of his rare grins.

"Now that's right, ma'am. Go on."

"But Uncle Gordon has a lot of faith in my judgment. And when I thought I might make the trip, to take care of Arthur, he said that was a splendid idea. When I got back I could give him a notion of what the place was like and whether it would be worth his while to try to break into that business."

"You—a woman?"

"I know it sounds silly, captain, but it must be that it's not. Because my Uncle Gordon is not a silly man."

"So I've always heard."

"If he sent one of his own men, a business man, the traders out there would all become clams. They'd make it hard for that man even to land. Maybe impossible. They're afraid of my Uncle Gordon. But nobody distrusts a helpless young woman."

Helpless!

"And he was too old to come out here himself," she added, "and anyway much too busy."

" I see. Then—you're not really a missionary after all. But I don't see why you didn't turn back when your brother died."

" Why didn't you turn back a little while ago? "

" Because I've got a job to do."

" Well, I've got two jobs to do. Uncle Gordon is entitled to his report. He paid for it—he ought to get it. And then there's my obligation to Arthur's memory. He meant to establish a mission in China. Well, I can't do that, and I probably wouldn't want to if I could. But what I can do is go to Canton and take a good look around for the L.M.S. people, and make them a full report, the same as I'm doing for Uncle Gordon. I think Arthur would have liked that.

" And now, captain," she said, looking up with a smile, " do we sort of understand one another better? "

" We do, Miss Mackenzie." He hooked an arm at her. " And to prove it, may I give myself the great pleasure of showing you over the ship? "

Gravely she laid a hand in the crook of his elbow. "Why, I would admire very much to see your ship, captain. Thank you."

Chapter Five

In the shipyard at Portersville, Connecticut, where he had once worked as an apprentice sawyer, Abner had been known as the most *un*nervous man the Lord ever created.

Stolid, expressionless, he believed in getting things done; and you can not get things done if you're going to go fussing and clucking around like a hen that has mislaid one of her chicks.

It was characteristic of Ab that he did not care for cursing—not because it shocked him but because it was so much wasted effort. When he ate he ate thoroughly and in silence, chewing his food well. Similarly his sleep was sound; he did not squirm or toss; and when he was finished he woke up all over, as a sailor should.

This is not to say that he never worried. He did. He had a great deal of feeling inside; but to let your anxiety show was, in his way of thinking, a womanish trait.

His first sleep after the sailing from Singapore was a full four-hour trick, and when he was awakened he began without pause to think about his troubles. He did this even while he was tugging on his boots.

All the way from Calcutta he had been troubled about the opium cargo they'd taken on there. Abner was not a superstitious man, but there were a good many stories in that part of the world about what happened to adventurers who carried the stuff. The profits were enormous, granted; yet the risks also were great, and men said that there was a curse upon the trade. The John Company itself, possibly for political reasons, wouldn't touch it, but left this business to the ships of a host of smaller, technically independent concerns known out East as "country companies". Even these had more than their share of trouble; but when some avaricious outsider, such as, say, Captain Thompson, gave the commerce a fling—then there was apt to be disaster. The ships of such skippers had a way of never being heard of again.

Well, Abner was committed to it. The stuff was in his charge and he would do his best to deliver it, and on time, ahead of the *Firefly*, which carried the same cargo.

More immediately, he thought as he pulled on the left boot, there was the matter of Miss Mackenzie. Carrying any kind of female, in the East anyway, was considered unlucky. Likewise, carrying a missionary was bad luck, maybe even more so. And while it was true that Miss Mackenzie was not actually a missionary, still the association was there. To find yourself, he thought angrily as he pulled on the right boot, with a passenger who happened to be both a missionary *and* a woman—this in addition to the curse that might well have been on the vessel because of the nature of her cargo——

Well, Ab didn't like it. He didn't like it at all.

Anne Mackenzie certainly was not a psalm-singing sister; and that much at least was a relief. But if a merchant of the calibre of Sir Gordon Mackenzie insisted upon sending a female scout to the other side of the world, why couldn't she, in all reason, be what you'd have expected a missionary to be—that is, some spinster of forty-odd, with a moustache, blackening teeth, and breastworks that suggested a collapsed tent?

The Lascars up forward were in a savage mood and couldn't be counted upon. The Chinese were reliable in most respects, but Abner had never heard that Oriental men had any different organs from their Caucasian counterparts; and in the next few weeks those hands and tindals were going to see a great deal of Anne Mackenzie—with the wind on her. Always there were but two officers. Paul Palmer was a large lad, strong as an ox, and utterly loyal; but still, he was only one man. What if Pooch got sick or was hurt? For that matter, what if Abner himself got hurt?

He was still shaking his head when he climbed to the deck, where Miss Mackenzie tossed him a broad, warm smile.

"Did you have a good sleep, captain? It's glorious up here."

He regarded her glumly. "Better pull that cloak around you," he said finally. "You'll get wet with the spray."

"About those account books——"

"Later," said Ab.

He checked the course, striving not to let his eyes stray to where she stood. Why did she have to be there? Why couldn't she be sick, like every other passenger he'd ever heard of?

He hoped he had not seemed overly impressed by the circumstance that she was Sir Gordon Mackenzie's niece. He had no wish to be one of those commercial snobs who prated of their acquaintance with this shipowner or that manufacturer, as obnoxious as the social satellites who let you know, every chance they got, that they were intimate with Lord This or Lady That. All the same, the connection in this case was not an easy one to ignore. Sir Gordon had a long arm.

Ab regarded the sea, which was making up. *Firefly* was still in sight, nearer now, yet less readily seen because of the pitching seas. Then he turned his attention to his own ship's canvas, and then the forward deck and the waist.

There were not many hands on watch. There were, indeed, suspiciously few. Even allowing for hangovers, there should have been more men up from the forecastle. What were they doing down there?

There was plenty of work for those who did appear. A surly lot, given to dark mutterings, they moved only when they had to, and glowered when shouted at. They tended to congregate in the waist, but Abner broke them up, barking. He was careful never to turn his back on them.

Pooch already had ordered all stunsail booms got in off the yards; and now Ab, in addition to shortening sail, had the topgallant masts lowered, the jib booms rigged in, the stern Moses hoisted onto the poop, and all the hatches battened down.

This took some time, and he did not once glance at Anne Mackenzie; all the same, he knew that she had not moved.

"Looks like we're going to get some weather," he remarked.

He was standing by the mainmast when he said this. The next instant, as he reached into his pocket for a cigar, an iron belaying pin whistled downwards past his face. It clicked against the buttons of his fearnaught and crashed to the deck at his feet.

He stared at it, the cigar halfway to his teeth. It was a common enough article—on deck. But why should anybody take a belaying pin aloft? There could be only one answer.

Forest was a bark, and her mizzen was lateen-rigged. Therefore, when the officers were aft, as they ordinarily were, there would be nobody working above them. It was different in the waist and forward, since both the other masts were square-rigged.

There were three men reefing on the maintops right now, Ab knew. Three Lascars. Anyone of these could have dropped the belaying pin. Ab's impulse was to order them down and to smash their faces one by one as they reached the deck, but he restrained himself. For one thing, he was seriously short-handed already. For another, he was not at all sure whether the rest of the crew would witness another beating, however much deserved, and not interfere.

They all had knives. He should not forget that fact.

He looked around. Everybody on deck, he saw, was silently watching him. Abner picked up the belaying pin. He slipped it casually into a pocket of his fearnaught. He stepped to the starboard scuppers, where he squatted, and in the lee of the gunnel there he lit his cigar with one of the new-fangled oxo-muriatic sulphur sticks.

"Aye," he repeated to nobody in particular as he headed aft, "it sure looks like nasty weather ahead."

Chapter Six

VAST THOUGH the ocean was, they lived in a small world.

That Abner and Pooch were obliged to share a cabin was no inconvenience, for they were used to narrow quarters and they were never in there at the same time anyway. How Anne Mackenzie was making out, with a chest of passenger cargo in addition to her personal effects, they did not know. She never complained; and day after day she emerged from that cabin a miracle of trim delight.

It was in the dining saloon that they really felt cramped. This was the only other room in the after quarters. It was at the end of the doll's-house passage, on either side of which were the cabins. It would seat three, just barely. The waiter—the skipper's striker, a Tamil boy named Yok—had to lean in through the doorway. The dining-saloon contained three small seats that folded back against the bulkhead when not in use and a small square let-down table. Because the weather made it difficult for the cook to keep his galley fire going, up forward, and doubly difficult for Yok to carry the meals aft, they all three ate at once.

In that place inevitably, time after time, whether below the table or above, they touched one another, knee to knee, thigh to thigh. This embarrassed Pooch Palmer, who most of the time appeared to be trying to hold his breath, an effort that made him subject to hiccups. He bolted his food. He seldom spoke, and when he did it was in gasps.

As for Abner, he guessed he liked conversation well enough—it depended, naturally, on whom it was with—and he knew that he liked eating; but it never had occurred to him to combine these two occupations. In his mind that made about as much sense as trying to play chess while you were taking a bath.

Anne Mackenzie kept things going. No chatterbox, still she could always find something to say. She sat between them, though neither of them ever looked at her; and they liked to listen to her—liked the sound of her crisp Scottish burr. She never whined, never talked through her nose. There was nothing uppish about her. She did not disapprove of things. It is true that she did ask Abner, before their first meal together, if he would remember to say grace each time; but he had been glad enough to promise this. No other note of religion was sounded.

On the other hand, and despite Anne Mackenzie's efforts, they were not very spirited occasions, those meals.

The lady's easy talk did not mislead Abner Smith, who put it down in part to good manners and in part to a natural shyness which she sought to conceal. Of one thing he was certain: though she might rattle on, here was no empty-headed fool. Anne's amiability was by no means all of her. Underneath it Abner sensed a will of iron. After all, this girl had elected to give up home and comfort, a secure position, to go halfway around the world, alone, to a forbidden land. He was not likely to forget the look that had come into her eyes when he said that he might put back.

And Abner sensed coming trouble with Anne Mackenzie. As on a perfectly clear day he sometimes would hear an inner storm signal, so there in the *Forest of Arden*'s minute dining saloon he was aware of breakers ahead— breakers not yet sighted or heard but none the less inevitably on their way. Hell, he knew, was due.

It was in the dining saloon that Abner did his calculations and pricked his chart, his own cabin being too small; and it was there too, between meals, that Anne Mackenzie went over the ship's books.

It was on the third day before he handed those books to her. There were several reasons for the delay. The weather continued bad, keeping Ab busy, and incidentally making navigation just that much harder, since he could not shoot the sun, though he kept careful track of—and in fact they were creeping up on—the brig *Firefly*, out of Boston, Mass. Then, too, Abner himself yearned for a good long study of those accounts. He was especially eager to learn the prices of things out here in the East. Finally,

Ab had not fully forgiven the lady for failing to make known her sex before sailing. He felt that, in a way, she had made a fool of him. She might be easy on the eyes, quick with her smile, and obliging, yet he resented her. Let her wait.

When he did hand over the accounts, however, he was pleased by the way she treated them. She had a real talent for mathematics. And she was thorough.

" Now, some of this silver is listed as bar silver and some is described as Sycee silver. Just what is Sycee silver? "

" Well, it's a matter of the form it comes in. Bar silver's bars. Sycee silver's always done up in the form of a small woman's slipper. No difference in the quality or the price."

" But—why like a slipper? "

" Hanged if I know, ma'am."

" I should think that, in a business like this, room would be an important consideration. Wouldn't silver shaped like small slippers take up more space than the same amount of silver stacked in bars? "

" Come to think of it, I guess it does."

" So I should think that if you were given the choice it would be better to ask for payment in bar silver, wouldn't it? "

" You know, that's just what I am going to do after this. Thank you, ma'am."

It was not silver, however that brought about the explosion in the dining saloon of the *Forest of Arden*. It was the rest of the cargo.

She called to him from the dining saloon the fourth morning out, as he was about to go topside and take over.

" Could I ask you something, captain? "

They sometimes did confer, for they shared an interest in accounts, in prices, rebates, taxes, port fees. He would lean over her where she sat, provocatively close, smelling her hair, her breath, and her body, while he explained something in the ledgers, this sometimes leading to a discourse on business practices in the East, greatly different from those in the western counting-houses. In this way he had told her about the commercial establishments at Singapore, Calcutta, Penang, Malacca; about the godowns, or warehouses, and factories of Canton, which were English, Dutch, French, Swedish, Portuguese, even American; about the Chinese customs laws. He told her about the extraordinary honesty of the Hong merchants, about million-dollar "teacup agreements" carefully carried out without a word of writing, and also about the appalling corruption of the port officials, and the inevitable and often too-severe "squeeze" or bribe that accompanied every request for a favour. He told her about the disadvantages of dealing with the larger established firms.

"Not for me. Too much what's-your-family or where-d'ye-come-from. Too many dead men's shoes. I'll start up for myself, if I ever do at all."

She had nodded. "Still," she'd said thoughtfully, "a good connection back home certainly wouldn't do you any harm."

"No, that's true enough."

On this particular morning, however, Abner Smith smelled trouble, serious trouble. They should be close to the *Firefly* now, steadily creeping upon her, and he wanted to crack on every inch of canvas the bark would take—everything but the cook's shirt, as the expression went. For this he would need hands. Not all hands maybe, but most of them. But where were they? And where had they been? Twice the previous day he had asked Kok Soo why so few of the Lascars were reporting on watch, and the answers had been evasive, the *serang* pretending that he did not understand all of Ab's English.

Ab had decided that unless there was a full roster to-day he would personally go down into the forecastle and find out what the matter was. That meant taking his life in his hands. He knew this, and it could be that the knowledge made him a bit edgy; he was gruff when he spoke to Miss Mackenzie.

"In a little while," he said. "I'll be back."

He put a foot on the ladder.

"But, captain——"

He pretended not to hear. He went up the ladder. They had been taking on a great deal of spray and even some green water, so the hatch was closed. He reached up and slid it open. He put his head above the level of the deck and——

The knife that was thrown at him did not actually touch his cheek, though he thought for an instant that it had. He gasped, freezing. He'd been given no chance to duck. He heard the *slish* past his left ear, heard also the *clunk* of the knife as it sank into the cover. Rolling his eyes, he saw the thing tremble there, inches from his cheek.

He had felt at the same instant a sting of pain, as though his cheek had been touched by a white-hot iron. The knife had knocked a fistful of splinters out of the cover, and some had flown into Abner's face. He reached up and pulled at them.

The ladder faced aft. The knife had come from behind Ab as he climbed. Before him now there was only a helmsman, one of the Chinese tindals, who was not looking down at the compass but up at the sky while he hummed a low, inane song. There was no sign of Pooch Palmer, who was on watch, but Abner could hear Pooch's voice. Pooch was forward, no doubt having seized some excuse for stretching his legs. Clearly, since he went on cursing somebody, he had not seen the knife thrown.

Abner whirled. He had not really hoped to see the man who threw the knife, nor did he. There were four Lascars working in the waist. Any one of them, knowing that Abner was about to come on watch, could have thrown the knife. None glanced up now. And behind Ab the helmsman went on singing softly, innocently, monotonously.

No doubt about it now, he'd have to have this out with the men—all of them. He'd have to have a show-down.

Pooch saw him and came striding towards him, waving excitedly. "I was going to call you. Look!"

Abner had already seen. Despite his rage, his instincts were functioning. Even while pulling the knife out, he had swiftly scanned canvas, sky, sea. The sight of the *Firefly* so jolted him that for a split-second he almost forgot his rage.

The brig from Boston was amazingly near, not much more than a mile away. To Abner it was incredible that the *Forest* had so lessened the distance between the two since the past sunset. And now he saw that the *Firefly* had very little canvas spread, no more than jibs and royals. Why? The weather was bad, but not that bad. There was no threat of a really hard blow. The seas were running high, but they weren't choppy. And the skipper of *Firefly* —that black-browed man named MacHarg, whom Ab with excellent reason hated like poison—was scarcely one to be over-cautious. He never would have got the berth if he had been.

Did they wish to speak to the *Forest of Arden*? Abner could not imagine why. But if that was the case, in half an hour or so it looked as though they'd have their chance.

In spite of his anger, Ab decided to put off that visit to the forecastle—for a little while. But only for a little while. The Lascars must be faced, and full on. There must be no more leniency. He would make every effort to find the man who threw that knife, probably the same one who had dropped the belaying pin; and if he did so he'd have him well and publicly beaten, no matter what the consequences. Even if he failed in this detection, he would at least learn what it was that kept so many of the crew out of sight below decks.

He took a deep breath. He had been scared in the first seconds after the knife was thrown. Now all he knew was fury, which shook him so that he trembled. And when Pooch reached him and asked him if everything was all right, he had to wet his lips twice and clear his throat before he could try to answer. He never quite got it out, however, because Anne Mackenzie, her voice almost harsh with anger, was suddenly lashing him from below for having walked away from her, for not staying to answer some very important questions she'd been saving up for him.

He said nothing in reply. It had occurred to him that the dining saloon might, for a little while, be the best place for him. He could get a grip on himself there, so that he'd be better prepared for the descent into the forecastle, for the dangerous confrontation of the crew. A little talk with Miss Mackenzie might do him a world of good. And when he came back on deck they might be near enough to *Firefly* to see what was going on over there.

"Keep the watch a little longer, mister," he said to Pooch.

Then he went below.

"This item, captain. Here——"

He read over her shoulder: *Calcutta, India, Sept. 16, Anno Dom. 1835, for owners 232 Chsts Malwa @ $825.00. . . . $92,400.00. For self, 8 chsts, same @ same. . . . $6,600.00.*

"That must represent a good part of our capacity, captain?"

"It's about half, yes."

"But isn't that expensive?"

"I'd call it right cheap. For one thing, you notice there that Captain Thompson invested in eight chests of it for himself. Now Andy Thompson isn't putting out any sixty-six hundred dollars unless he gets a real buy—and all this has to be cash, of course. Theoretically he's supposed to stow that in his own cabin, but actually you couldn't even get one whole chest in there, much less eight. But that's what he's allowed, for his own private adventure. One of the skipper's prerogatives. Just like you're allowed, as a passenger, to carry a chest or sack of something for trading purposes. That's ground ginseng you got in that chest in your cabin, isn't it?"

She shook her head with impatience. It must have seemed to her that Abner was tending to evade her question.

"But—what *is* Malwa, that it costs so much?"

"Oh, it's the very best there is. The best money can buy. Far better than that Turkish stuff."

"The very best *what*?"

"Why, mud."

"*Mud*?"

"Why, yes, mud. That's what they call it. Opium."

That last word was the crack of a whip. She stiffened. Her eyes, always large, showed as hard as ice.

"Captain, do you mean to tell me that we have *opium* aboard?"

"Sure. That's our load, mostly. Mud. We don't carry it regular, but I suppose Andy Thompson just couldn't resist the temptation. After all, you don't often get a chance to buy real Malwa at any price. Mostly the rajahs keep it for themselves."

"Filthy stuff!"

"Oh, no, it's the finest there is."

"Am I to understand that without any orders from your owners you took it upon yourself to deal in this vicious drug?"

Now she was acting more like a missionary might be expected to act, and Abner didn't like it.

"Not at all. Andy Thompson did. He was entirely within his rights. A bargain's a bargain no matter where you get it."

"But you knew the nature of the cargo, before you took over command at Singapore?"

"Oh, sure. I supervised the stowage. That's part of a first mate's job. I was the first then."

He was trying to control his temper. Actually, he did not like the idea of running opium, but he wasn't going to be lectured about it—especially by a female Scot.

"Don't you see, ma'am, it's my duty to make as much as I possibly can for the owners, and I'll get maybe as much as two thousand dollars a chest for that stuff in China."

"What will you get for the souls of the men it ruins?"

He shrugged. "Opium ain't so bad. Ever seen a man under the influence of it?"

"Certainly not!"

"I have. Heaps of times. I've hauled 'em out of more dens than you could shake a bamboo pipe at. They're not bad. They're foolish. They—they're *fuzzy*. But they're always pleasant. They grin at you, even when you hit 'em. I'd rather handle a dope than a drunk any night. They can be mighty silly sometimes, but I don't reckon their immortal souls change."

"Captain, I believe you smoke opium yourself!"

"No, ma'am. I did try it once, just to see what it was like, but all it did was give me a headache. Besides, it costs so much."

She rose. "That wasn't amusing, captain."

"Maybe it wasn't meant to be."

She slammed shut the ledger. "And I may say here and now that I refuse to do anything further towards helping out such a business."

"Suit yourself," he said, and he picked up the ledger and took it back to his own cabin.

When he came out in the passage again she was waiting for him.

"At the very least, captain, may I remind you that smuggling narcotics into China happens to be against the law?"

"We don't smuggle it. Somebody else does that. We

simply dump it into the floating godowns at Lintin, those hulks I told you about. What happens to it after that is none of our concern. Another way they sometimes do is they run up the coast until some pirates board you and seize the cargo."

" But I thought—the guns——"

" These are a different kind of pirates. They pay for what they take. And they pay more than the men in the floating godowns. They can afford to. It saves them a lot of squeeze. Saves a middleman, see? But they're pirates, all right! It says so right on their shirts. It says 'very fierce pirate' or maybe 'frightfully ferocious pirate'. In Chinese, of course."

" No doubt this is very funny, captain, but I don't see it that way."

" Of course, they *might* turn out to be the real thing. That's a chance you take."

" The way I see it is that a man I used to trust and respect has confessed that he has a hand in the world's dirtiest traffic. Even *boasted* about it."

This was too much. He turned on her.

" Coming from you, Miss Mackenzie, who's got a whole chest of ground ginseng in her cabin——"

" What's the matter with ground ginseng? "

" That's Nepalese you got. You know what they use that for? "

" No. What? "

He stifled a chuckle.

" They brew it into some kind of tea, don't they? " she asked.

" Sometimes. The *men* do. But not because they like the taste of it. To them it's nothing but a—— Well, I don't know how you pronounce that word, but anyway they take it so's they'll be stronger. In bed, I mean."

She slapped his face.

It felt good. He nodded, and turned. He was humming when he went up on deck again.

Chapter Seven

THE WIND had picked up, and the seas were running long and high, with strips of spitting foam at their crests. The deck was wet. Spume that stung like needles filled the air.

" Better let me go," Pooch shouted to Ab.

"No. You stay here. And if I don't come up again— send one of the Chinese for me, don't go for me. We can't afford to lose both our officers."

Pooch spat. "God damn the old man," he said slowly and with feeling.

There was no need for Ab to ask whom he meant. Andrew Thompson was lying in the home of a Singapore friend, recovering his strength; but his spirit still stalked the *Forest of Arden*. Thompson was a good skipper, from the owners' point of view. He got things done. He showed a profit. But the hands hated him. The original crew of the *Forest* had deserted to a man when Calcutta was reached, and it was there that the Chinese and the Lascars had been signed on. Afterwards there had been one flogging after another, so that scarcely a man in the forecastle did not carry on his back criss-cross weals to remind him of his captain. The second mate, too—he and his rattan had not been forgotten.

All this was no fault of Ab Smith and Pooch Palmer. But it was too late to do anything about it now.

The forecastle, which Abner proposed to visit, was a narrow, cramped, and very dark place. It was the exclusive home of the hands. At any time intrusion there by an officer would have been resented. In the present circumstances . . .

Ab gave a hitch to his belt, checked the course, then nodded towards the *Firefly*. "But first we'll find out what MacHarg wants," he decided.

The sight of the brig from Boston soothed him somewhat. He had no love for *Firefly* and her tyrannical master, but she was a splendid thing, smart, fast, efficient, every inch a Yankee ship. You saw so many sloppy, stinking craft out East that such a meeting as this, even with an arch rival, was a welcome change.

It could have been that Ab's feeling was not unmixed with complacency. He commanded what he believed would be the winner. Despite *Firefly's* head start, despite her full complement of officers and men—and Abner sighed at the sight of all those sailors—he was sure *Forest of Arden* was the better ship.

Abner, watching the other, felt a father's pride in his own ship. *Firefly* was speedy, granted. On her taller sticks she could spread more canvas. But a great deal of this was "small" canvas—stunsails, royals, flying jibs, sprit-sails—that would have to come down in any kind of blow. *Firefly* could not make about as handily as *Forest*. On the North Atlantic run, the passage to Liverpool, it might have been different. There her superior spread before a steady wind would have given the Boston vessel an advantage. But in these waters, and especially at this season, beating up against the monsoon, tacking, tacking, it should be *Forest of Arden*'s race, he felt.

This made it the more curious that *Firefly* should throw away what little lead she did have. Clearly it was Mac-Harg's purpose to speak to the Stonington vessel. He was only a few cable lengths ahead, a few points off the starboard bow. Soon *Forest* would come alongside, at which time *Firefly* could crowd on canvas, if she wished, and keep up for a space. Abner had no intention of shortening sail. Time was money, and he had a job to do, goods to deliver.

What *did* MacHarg want? He could not be checking his position, for he had been heard to declare publicly what he thought of Andy Thompson—whom he would suppose still in command of the *Forest*—when it came to navigation, an art in which MacHarg was an acknowledged expert. Water? Wood? It was unlikely, only five days out of port. A gam, or nautical conversation, a mid-ocean chat? Vessels did that from time to time, especially Yankee vessels in far-off places. But MacHarg could not be called a sociable man. Did he have some important news? If so, when did he get it? Except after sundown and when there was rain, those aboard the *Forest* had kept the brig in sight all the time, and it was virtually certain that she had spoken no other vessel.

Ab frowned, fingering the knife in his pocket.

Anne Mackenzie came up from below. She held a scoop of ground Nepalese ginseng root. She emptied this over the lee rail. Pooch Palmer stared in astonishment. Abner pretended not to see her, as she pretended not to see him. But she slipped on the wet deck as she passed, and would have fallen had he not caught her.

"Thank you," she said coldly, and brushed herself off.

He touched his cap, his eyes straight ahead. She went below, presently to appear with another scoopful of ginseng.

This was too much for Pooch. It was evident that she was methodically throwing the stuff away, the chest being too heavy for her to haul up on deck. The mate started towards Anne.

"See here, can't I give you a hand with that?"

She paused, about to smile, about to thank him, when Abner cut in.

"Better stick to your post, mister. Remember, you're on watch."

He could have bitten his tongue off the next instant. It had been a petty remark. He felt his face going hot while he looked away, conscious that a confused Pooch Palmer was staring at him. But Anne Mackenzie smiled a slow, understanding, and quietly triumphant smile. It had been her round. The skipper had lost his temper.

Abner couldn't rescind the command. Neither could he apologize to Miss Mackenzie in Pooch's presence, or to Pooch in hers. What he would have done next he was never to know. Because just then all hell broke loose.

Abner Smith could not have been called a naïve seaman. He was no innocent. He knew all the tricks in his line of trade, dirty and otherwise. Suspicious by nature, no optimists, the men he lived among and did business with were fiercely competitive. Get the best price: this was all they asked. Methods didn't matter. It was coin planked down on the barrel-head. In consequence Ab Smith was not often off his guard. Even when he slept he slept with one ear open.

The possibility of a trick had occurred to him when it first became evident that *Firefly* was falling off. But— what trick? What could the Bostonian do?

He never considered the *Firefly*'s cannon. The brig mounted three carronades on each side, amidships, and a bow gun and stern chaser, swivel weapons. The carronades were broadside smoothbores in set positions. They could not be elevated or depressed, and they could be aimed only along with the ship that mounted them. In a sea like this they would be useless. Abner had heard before leaving Stonington that the U.S. Navy was ordering some of those new-fangled Armstrong guns from England, guns that were supposed to self-regulating against the roll of a ship at sea; but *Firefly* was no part of the Navy. Her carronades were unmanned now, and as the two vessels drew closer Ab Smith could see that a tompion or weather-plug had been thrust into the muzzle of each. As for the swivel guns, these too were unattended, and they were covered with tarpaulins.

Abner had been alert. There was nothing he could reproach himself for. The trick had been well planned, as it was beautifully executed. No skipper in his right mind could have been expected to provide against it.

There was a man on the poop of the *Firefly* who held a speaking trumpet. He was tall, strong, Abner's own build, and arrogant in manner. He was the only officer in sight, which in itself was strange. As the vessels neared he kept shouting at Abner to get closer—kept shouting too that he couldn't hear what Abner replied, though Ab could hear him and the wind was at Ab's back. In any event, Abner had no thought of getting closer. They were already too close for comfort, in his opinion, and he shouted as much. The man with the speaking trumpet shouted back that he couldn't hear.

Abner, exasperated, refused to continue the colloquy.

The vessels were now side by side. Scarcely two hundred feet separated them. Pooch was at the wheel. In part because of his uneasiness, but in part too because he was trying to recover from his embarrassment before Anne Mackenzie, Abner was about to give an order to change course slightly—when he saw the man with the speaking trumpet step back, turning his head to look down a cabin hatch as he did so.

Suddenly on both poop and forward deck of the *Firefly* men appeared, seemed to spring miraculously out of thin air—though they must have been lying in the scuppers, concealed from sight by the gunnel. Obviously they had been well rehearsed. In an instant they had torn the tarpaulins off the swivel guns. These guns had no tompions! They were ready to fire. On each deck one of the men had a tub with a slow-match. Abner gave a great shout and twisted the wheel in Pooch Palmer's hands. *"Down!"* He threw himself against a petrified Anne Mackenzie, knocking her to the deck, and then sprawled full length upon her.

That was when the first crash came.

Chain shot! It could be nothing less. Chain shot, essentially a naval battle ammunition, was effective only at short range. The conditions here were ideal. The small steel balls, each pair joined by a length of chain, went whistling through the air—to slash the running gear of *Forest of Arden* like so many aerial fiends.

The effect was electric. The bark seemed to rear like a frightened horse. The deck shivered, and there was a thunderous noise in the rigging—the prime target of the chain shot.

Sails or sections of sails, cut loose, flapped and crackled. Spars fairly screamed, like living things, when they were hit; and they spewed splinters in all directions. The very masts seemed to groan under the impact.

A moment later, severed ropes, ratlines, slats, booms pelted down onto the deck. It was against this that Abner had hurled himself on top of Anne Mackenzie, and they were not hit.

Ab raised his head. All this had happened very fast, yet already the *Firefly* was moving ahead, her hands feverishly spreading canvas, while the bark from Stonington staggered like a crippled elk, falling away.

Ab ducked again as the second shot was fired, the one from the poop. It was deafening, worse than the first. Once again there was a shattering rain of material. Had the decks been crowded, or even reasonably occupied—instead of being almost deserted, as if the *Forest* were a plague ship—somebody surely would have been killed. Abner did hear a screech of pain that he was later to learn came from a Lascar whose ankle had been smashed; but that was all. Luck.

He rose. *Forest* had no way on her, the wheel swung idle. The deck was a shambles. From the onsurging *Firefly*, already too far off for another shot, came a low, derisive laugh.

Abner helped Anne Mackenzie to her feet. He knew

that he was trembling, and knew that he had been frightened; but he could not help thinking, even then, that part of his feeling might be accounted for by the fact that he had just been lying on top of a lovely woman.

She too must have been frightened. Yet there was a glint of mockery in her eyes.

" Is this the way Americans greet one another when they meet on the other side of the world? "

" Apparently some do," he said shortly.

" Thank you," she went on more gravely, " for saving my life."

She swayed towards him and might, in her great relief have thanked him more warmly, but he only mumbled something and turned away. After watching him for a moment, she went below.

It could be supposed that after two such terrific explosions and the clatter of falling gear and the loss of way, the crew would come boiling up out of the forecastle to see what had happened. Nothing of the sort. Arms akimbo, Ab Smith surveyed the damage; it would take at least a couple of days to repair it. Picking himself up from behind the wheel was the Chinese tindal, who no longer sang. Pooch stood blinking, dazed. In the waist were four frightened Lascars, including the one with the smashed ankle. Abner glanced towards the forecastle hatch. Nothing stirred there.

" That settles it," he snapped. " Now we'll have it out."
He started forward.

" Are you going to call them up? " Pooch asked.

" *Call* them up? Mister, I'm going to *bring* them up ! "

Chapter Eight

I T W A S like descending into Hell.

Abner Smith, like anybody else from Stonington who had been properly brought up, often thought about Satan's domain. Abner, though, had never pictured it in his mind as a *hot* place. Quite the contrary, to him it had always suggested something clammy, dank. Many a time in meeting-house he had the conventional limbo of lost souls described; and he guessed he believed in it all right, because it would be a sin to disbelieve anything that was in the Book. But—it just wasn't *his* Hell. He had his own.

As he saw it, and felt it, for all the horror of seething brimstone, for all the boiling lakes, the red-hot pincers, the howling of the damned, and the everlasting laceration of the flesh, for all this, the simple fact remained that where there was so much flame there must be plenty of light; and Abner calculated that man's worst enemy was, rather, darkness. So it was that he thought of Hell as a swamp, a sewer, a noisome cellar, where snakes slithered and toads squatted, an abominable place through which a disembodied soul would stumble fearsomely, arms outstretched, his skin crimped with the cold, his feet sliding in slime; while wet cold hands, hands he could not see, caressed him in unusual places, or slapped him, or dug into him; and somewhere near at hand would be a low, tittering, malicious laugh.

58

Above all, he thought of Hell as a place that *stank*. And the forecastle certainly did that.

Abner's knee joints might have been made of lard as he slid back the forecastle hatch; but he took pains that this condition should not show.

He was not afraid of anything he could face, but turning his back would take real guts. More than half the crew was down there. Nine or ten of them. They could see him coming, legs first, see him silhouetted against the hatchway, and for a long moment they would have him at the mercy of their knives.

He swallowed hard.

The hatch had been kept closed as a matter of course in seas like these, yet likely enough it would have been shut even in a calm. Sailors were men who got too much fresh air while at work and they preferred it stale and stench-laden when they were at leisure.

"Stand aside down there. This is the captain."

The bad odours rose in a concentrated cloud, seeming fairly to smite him, like some physical substance, like steam or smoke. It was a miasma made up of sweat, rancid oil, sea water, dirt, squashed bugs, urine, and the sour smell of vomit—but there was something else as well, something less readily expected, more insidious.

Abner went down.

There was no unmannerly scramble, which might have been taken as a sign of weakness, something he couldn't afford; but he did not waste any time either.

When he got to the bottom he turned around.

Though the day was anything but bright, yet going down into the forecastle had been like leaving brilliant sunshine for the dimness of a cave.

At first he could see nothing at all. Then bunks to right and left loomed as a vague blur. Just in front, swinging back and forth by a chain, was a whale-oil lamp.

Soon he began to make out eyes, many of them. He was surrounded by them; and they were evil-lit, it seemed, glaring at him. They did not look human. They rocked in the rocking light of the lamp, while small sly shadows flitted along the wall.

From here and there, uncertainly, never from one fixed place, came a susurrous stirring, no more than the suggestion of a whisper. It might have been a million moths batting their wings against a window. Somebody giggled —a silken sound, very soft. Somebody gulped.

Ab took a short forward step. So thick was the air that it felt as if he had walked into a faceful of cobwebs, and with an impatient gesture he brushed his hand across his forehead.

He had identified the unexpected odour, and it made him furious. This was good for him. It stung like acid on an open wound, causing him to forget his fear.

" *Who's been into the cargo?* "

He took a step forward. He unhooked the lamp. He held it now this way, now that, examining the faces of those who lay in the bunks.

They did not try to avoid his glare. Rather, with a single exception, they beamed foolishly up at him. One of them even started to sing, a blubbered monotonous melody that stopped when Abner slapped him with the back of his hand; and even after that, even while blood swam up through his teeth and spilled over his lips, the man smiled on and on.

The exception was the tiny bundle-of-rags Abner and

Andy Thompson had shanghaied. Ab remembered hauling him out of the Singapore bunk and thinking as he
did so that here was no more than a boy. He remembered
the den proprietor's shrill protest, and how he had marvelled at it. Just now the bundle-of-rags lay flat on his
face, his slim bare arms curled over his head, the rest of
him as shapeless as before. Ab had never seen him on deck,
now that he thought of it. Here he was miles and miles
away, hours away, in some never-never land. A pipe lay
on the floor beside him, and next to that was a ball of
black, lustreless, slightly moist stuff that might have been
drying mud; it was about the size of Abner's fist, a large
one, and it had been wrapped in dark-green, smooth-edged
leaves, now partly peeled back.

Abner Smith picked this up. He rewrapped it, shaking
his head. Real Malwa, meant for princes! No wonder
these hands, accustomed to the scrapings of third-class
pipes, had found it too rich for them. Ab pocketed it
carefully.

He decided, coldly, that he would have at least one of
them flogged, and well flogged, as an example. He would
dock them half their pay, and he would prohibit any sort
of shore leave, for whatever reason, when they reached the
anchorage near Canton.

It was against Kok Soo that his anger was chiefly
directed. He knew that Kok had not indulged: Abner
would have smelled it on him. But the bos'n surely had
known what was going on—nobody could so much as stick
his head inside that forecastle hatchway and not know—
and it was his duty to report. Ab as skipper had been
liberal about hangovers. But when they were so short-
handed, and running into weather, to permit such

shenanigans after the first twenty-four hours was nothing short of criminal. Kok Soo would pay.

But how had they got the stuff? Every chest had been stored in the main hold, and this was accessible only through the Number 1 and Number 2 hatches. Both these hatches had been battened down after the stowage at Calcutta, Abner himself supervising the job. Except when the two officers ate together, the only time the hatches had not been in sight of an officer since that time was the two hours just before sailing from Singapore, when West had been taken ashore with fever, Captain Thompson was making last-minute arrangements, and Abner and Pooch were rounding up members of the crew; and that, cer-tainly, what with all the rest of the work that was done then, would not have permitted the bos'n or anybody else to break open a hatch, extricate one of those closely packed chests—they weighed almost three hundred pounds apiece—smash the lock, rifle the chest, put it back, and replace the hatch and batten it down again. No, it wasn't possible. There must be some other explanation.

He turned, raising his lamp, and, no longer fearful for his back, carefully examined the bulk head behind the ladder. Sweat poured down his body and he was all but suffocated by the fumes of the opium, but at last his hands found a loose board and he lifted this out.

It was the only loose board, the only one that had been tampered with. Abner got to his knees and reached in through the opening. His arm was long, but though he swung it in all directions it came upon nothing.

That meant that somebody had squeezed through this small space.

At first it seemed impossible. Nobody aboard was small enough. Then he remembered the bundle-of-rags.

He rose and turned, putting the lamp down. The muscles of his jaw twitched.

"*Kok Soo!*"

"Aye, aye, sir," came the voice of the Chinese *serang* from the deck.

Doubtless others were up there, crowded around the forecastle hatch. Well, the more the merrier. This lesson was going to be made to tell. It would be one they'd never forget.

"Fetch out the lash!"

"Aye, aye, sir."

Abner seized the ankles of the bundle-of-rags. With one mighty heave he hauled the little sleeper out of the bunk and threw him like a sack of salt up through the hatchway.

"*Stand by—I'm coming up!*"

Yes, the forward deck was crowded. Only the helmsman and Anne Mackenzie remained on the poop; and Anne, with a scoopful of ginseng in her hands, was picking her way towards the taffrail. She was stubborn, this Scotswoman. Regardless of bombardment, she was going to finish the job of jettisoning the stuff.

Abner paid no heed to the inert figure he had thrown up through the opening. He stepped right over it, and went for Kok Soo.

The Chinese did not flinch. He knew what was about to happen. He wore a sheath knife, but his hand never moved towards its hilt.

"*You* knew what was going on!"

Abner punched him in the jaw.

Kok Soo staggered back, his arms limp at his sides. Ab went after him and hit him again, bringing the fist up from somewhere near the deck.

Kok Soo sat in the scuppers, and his head slammed back against the gunnel. His eyes were still closed. He gave a low moan.

Ab, standing astride of him, pointed back to the prone figure from the forecastle.

"Douse yourself in sea-water. Then, when you can stand up, have that fellow stripped and spread-eagled across the capstan. But don't whip him yet. Not until he can feel it—every bit of it."

The *serang* had opened his eyes, though these were glassy. He was trying to point to something on the deck— something past Abner's legs. He was trying to say something.

"I don't want explanations. You know your job. Do it, or I'll have you flogged too."

Kok Soo did not try to rise, perhaps fearing that Abner would knock him down again, but he kept pointing to a place beyond Abner's legs.

Abner turned, and saw what everybody else already had seen.

The bundle-of-rags was turned over the other way now, and many of those rags, sleazy at best, had been torn by Ab's handling and by violent contact with the deck. Not only was the whole chest laid bare but so was the belly, and farther down. . . .

It needed no anatomist to tell them that this was a woman.

"In God's name," and he said this reverently, not blasphemously, "what will we *do* with her?"

"As long as it *is* done in God's name, captain, does it matter?"

Anne Mackenzie had emerged from the waist. She climbed the ladder easily with one hand, still holding in the other the scoop of ginseng.

"We might start by covering her up decently," she said, as she started to take off her cloak.

Pooch put out a hand.

"But ma'am, she's a——"

"Shut up. She's got an immortal soul, hasn't she? Now get out of my way."

Abner Smith stepped forward.

"And you too," she snapped at him. "What do *you* know about women?"

She threw the ground ginseng into his face.

When Abner had cleared his eyes and stopped coughing, he saw that everybody was either looking at him, afraid to say anything, or else looking at Anne Mackenzie.

Easily carrying the doped, inert girl, Anne had reached the poop. She strode across this, holding her burden high, while the north-east monsoon found every curve in a body no longer cloaked.

Abner wiped a few additional grains of the aphrodisiac from his lips, and looked at them.

"No," he whispered. "No, I don't need this stuff."

E

Chapter Nine

T HERE WERE rain squalls all that morning, into the first of which the *Firefly* vanished. Had MacHarg, confident that he had badly crippled his rival, allotted himself more time for the run, and was he moving out of these waters, which were dangerously close to the Paracels? Abner did not know, nor did he have the time to wonder.

The wreckage on deck had looked somewhat worse than it proved to be; yet it was bad enough. Fortunately Abner, as first mate, had provided for accidents—though never expecting to be hit with chain shot—and the gear lockers were full. They carried two extra suits of sail, plus a great deal of cordage and spare spars. For all their shortcomings, the Lascars were tolerably good carpenters and extremely good needlemen, and quick at splicing. As the fumes wore off, one by one these men were hauled up on deck. For almost a week they had floated in a fragrantly exclusive paradise, lapped in loveliness and muted song, deliciously drowsing. Now, abruptly, they found themselves back on the job, with more work than ever. They didn't like it.

The work was back-breaking, yet it proceeded briskly and without let-up, the weather co-operating. The wind stayed from the north-east, but late in the morning it fell off until it was scarcely more than a breeze; and, as though declaring itself in accord with this attitude, the sea smoothed at the same time. The sky was clear and fair, the air dry. This was extraordinary at that season in the South China Sea. It was, in fact, too good to be true.

The spars had been badly knocked about, and one of the larger booms had slammed to the deck. The standing rigging was a mad tangle, but the running gear held, more or less. The masts themselves were chipped but as far as Ab could determine none of them had been overstrained. Oddly enough, the two worst casualties were the carronades in the waist. The falling boom had struck them fairly on top, mashing the touch-holes so badly that priming pins could no longer be plugged into them. A gunsmith with the proper kit could have rendered the weapons workable again within a few hours, but there was no gunsmith aboard the bark. The carronades still *looked* formidable, but they could not be fired.

The going being what it was, no more than one helmsman at a time was needed. The *Forest* still tacked, as doubtless she would be obliged to do throughout the whole run, but the putting about was not the strenuous stint it once had been. This gave the officers more opportunity to leave the after deck and supervise the work in the waist.

Abner had the Number 2 hatch opened. It was as he had guessed. One chest only had been violated, and but four balls were gone. Ab left this chest as he found it and ordered the hatch battened down again.

There was some doubt in his mind, for a while, as to what should be done about the yellow female. He had taken her from an illegitimate establishment; and though that place had been what the French call a *maison tolérée*, or tolerated house, yet it was the accepted practice, and a point of much importance in the Singapore underworld,

as Abner well knew, that in no circumstances whatever
should any manner of female be admitted to a public pipe-
house. No doubt this was why the proprietor, whose
doxie she doubtless was, had dressed her as a man: he
would not risk her out of his sight while he worked.

All of which meant that she had no official status. She
could not be traced. No one would stand responsible for
her. So—she might be hard to get rid of. And now?
Well, even though she had filched from the cargo and
corrupted the crew, Abner could not have her flogged, as
he had originally planned. First of all, she was a female,
however debased. Secondly, such a show might well lead
to her death—or to mutiny. Yet since she could not even
do the work of a boy, Abner was certainly not going to pay
her out of the ship's money, much less out of his own
pocket. And where would she sleep? He could not bunk
her forward, for sure as snakes she would cause trouble
among the crew and knives would be drawn. Yet if he
kept her aft, in the officers' quarters, that would look like
rewarding her for thievery and vice.

But if there was doubt in Abner's mind, there was none
in Anne's. Where the girl was concerned, *she* gave the
orders. In whatever category the others might put this
person who had stolen the opium—and Abner for one
thought of her as a stowaway, even though he himself had
kidnapped her and brought her aboard—to Anne she was
a woman who needed a friend. So it was that the yellow
girl remained in Anne's cabin.

There was a wide streak of the mother in Miss Mackenzie. She might have been a tigress defending her cub.
The rest of mankind did not greatly matter to her now,
except as she bossed it about. She no longer tried to keep

out of their way; her hope was that they would keep out of hers. She did not take the trouble to be cold, any more than she took the trouble to be sociable. Meals were less crowded, if less animated, with only Ab and Pooch in attendance; for the merchant prince's secretary had hers in her room, and she made a row when they were not exactly what she had stipulated or were not promptly served.

Her former table mates she treated much as she treated Yok the Tamil. They were there to wait on her, as Yok was, and she did not hesitate to call upon them. Whenever one of them had occasion to go along that narrow passage-way between the cabins he was likely to see her door opened while she commanded him to bring fresh towels or hot water, or she might hand out a bunch of dirty linen or a slop-jar or chamber-pot for emptying.

Sometimes Abner wondered what would happen when that little slut in there came back to life. How long this would take nobody knew, for it depended upon many things, though chiefly on two—the condition of her own constitution and the amount of narcotic she had smoked. Addicts, Ab knew, could go for days in a coma, scarcely aware of what was happening around them. This Chinese might, conceivably, still suppose herself to be in the den of her protector. She might have done the stealing and all the rest of it without ever emerging from her scented dream.

Surely she had never before been so clean and so well tended. Would she think herself in Heaven when she came to consciousness? If so it would be a cramped Heaven.

Ab and Pooch knew from the way she moved around

and from the requests she made that Anne Mackenzie was busy about many things—washing, nursing, mending, sewing. Sometimes they heard her talking, slowly, on a low pitch, to the little Chinese whore; but they never heard an answer.

Ab's first sight of the patient was on the second morning after her shift of quarters. Anne had opened her cabin door at the sound of his footstep, though he had tried to be quiet, and she was demanding that he get her a fresh mango, something they were out of. He tried to tell her this. He was trying to explain that you could not keep mangos more than a few days in these parts—not without ice anyway and of course they were thousands of miles from any ice.

His voice trailed off. The door behind Anne had swung fully open, and he saw the little Chinese. He caught his breath.

She was propped up in the lower bunk with more pillows than Abner had known the cabin contained. She was as clean as the bedclothes themselves. Her hair had been combed and oiled, and it was piled on the top of her small and shapely head. Her ears gleamed like alabaster. There was no powder on her face, but it needed none, for it showed luminous and clear, and the eyebrows were plucked to perfection. The eyes below those brows, mere slits, might have been painted in with a brush; Abner could not know whether she saw him, or saw anything.

She wore a crisp grey frock, obviously made over from one of Anne's, which nevertheless fitted her excellently. Her little hands, folded in her lap, had long nails—but no rings.

Placid, pallid, she sat without stir; and she might have

been an Oriental idol enshrined in a temple, except for two things—the absence of jewellery, and the suggestion, very faint, of a silly smile.

It was clear that Anne resented this glimpse of her charge.

"Her name is Shen Ti, and she says she is a princess, a Manchu princess."

"Most of 'em say that."

"But she has not really recovered yet."

"She's due for a shock when she does."

Anne turned. "This is the captain, Shen Ti," she said gently. "Captain Smith."

Abner removed his cap, he couldn't have said why.

"Pleased to meet you."

The idol did not move. Maybe it didn't hear?

"If she seems a little simple, it's your fault."

"Mine?"

"If it wasn't for mercantile greed," Anne Mackenzie expanded, "there wouldn't be pitiful children like her. All right—if you can't get us a mango, then bring us some tea."

The door was slammed.

Abner was thoughtful as he went for the tea. The sight of that slim creature propped in a bunk had strangely moved him. So had Anne Mackenzie's scorn.

Chapter Ten

T HE NEXT time he saw Shen Ti the circumstances were altogether different.

It was the following afternoon. He was off watch but lingering topside to check some jobs. Pooch, who had taken over, was seated on the taffrail watching the sun set and chatting with Anne—or rather, listening to her chat. Pooch had got over some of his original shyness with Anne, though still not exactly loquacious. Evidently the trollop was asleep below, for this was the first time Anne Mackenzie had appeared on deck since the storm. She ignored Abner.

Ab was tired. He checked the course, nodded, gazed a while at the setting sun, a highly flamboyant one, too red to please his sailor's eye, and then studied the limp, lifeless canvas. *Forest* had almost no way on her at all. Abner didn't like it. It was unnatural.

He sighed and went below.

The Chinese girl was lying in his bunk. She was not asleep, though her eyes, as they had been yesterday, were almost shut.

She lay on her back. Her shoulders and arms were bare. She was loosely covered by a Cashmere shawl—something Anne must have picked up in Calcutta—which oddly enough did not look incongruous on her. Her small bare feet and ankles showed below it.

When she saw him she smiled slowly, languidly, though all the time she did not seem to open her eyes.

"I am Shen Ti," she lisped. "You are the captain. You save me. Come."

Abner hung up his cap.

"You'd better get back to your own room," he mumbled.

She stirred, and the shawl, disturbed, slithered off. Now she was naked. She stretched out her arms.

"I make you happy," she whispered. "Come to Shen Ti."

Abner was agitated; but though blood pounded in his veins it was because of anger more than desire. There was a time and place for everything. After all, he was running a ship.

"Now, now, that's enough," he snapped. "You go back where you belong."

He wrapped the shawl around her and lifted her out of the bunk. She was not as light as he expected her to be, not sylphlike at all. A full and firm body was here in his arms. He wondered how he had ever plucked it out of that other, narrower, dirtier bunk and flung it away like a bundle of dirty laundry. She was warm against his chest. The clean, sweet smell of her was as heady as liquor. Her arms snaked around his neck.

Holding her tight, he kicked open the door and stepped out into the passageway—and found himself face to face with Anne Mackenzie.

Anne had never looked so lovely. Her eyes were ablaze as she snatched Shen Ti from Abner's arms and hustled her into her own cabin. She was back immediately.

"A lovely state of affairs," and her voice scraped like a fingernail on slate, "when even the captain of a ship practises seduction!"

"There was no seduction."

"But it was attempted!"

"Aye. But not by me."

"Are you implying that——"

"I'm not implying anything. I'm saying it. And I am also saying that if any passenger on this ship insists on dredging trulls up out of the gutter and treating them like a human being, then the least she could do is keep them from sneaking into other peoples' beds. Do I make myself clear?"

"You do. Disgustingly clear. What you are doing, captain, is accusing that innocent, misled girl——"

"*Innocent?* Look here, Miss Mackenzie. Never mind where I found her in the first place, but anyway she's been five days and nights in the forecastle along with more than a dozen sailors. What d'ye think they were doing all that time—playing dominoes?"

She puzzled him. He couldn't help himself. He saw her loneliness, as he admired her spunk. He sensed that if he put out a conciliatory hand, or even made his voice a bit milder, she might thaw considerably. He was almost sure of it. But still she rubbed him the wrong way.

Abner was not a quarrelsome man; quite the contrary. He had enough fights in the ordinary course of business without going out of his way to look for extra ones. But freeboard, and wide rudders, they were highly manœuvr-skipper.

"If she committed any sin," Anne said stiffly, "then she will be forgiven."

"Well, we can hope so, anyway."

"If she committed any sin down there it was because of you."

It was well that Captain Smith was not a swearing man.

He drew himself up. "Ma'am, I was not even in the fore-castle while that was going on."

"You know what I mean. You gave her the poison that corrupted her."

"I did nothing of the kind. She stole it."

"She didn't know what she was doing."

Abner jerked his head towards the door of his own cabin.

"Well, she knew what she was doing in there just now."

Anne trembled with the intensity of her rage, and her voice sounded as black and bitter as gall, if a little shaky: "I understood you to say, captain, that—that nothing happened in there just now."

"Nothing did, if you mean what I think you do. But it wasn't *her* fault that it didn't."

"This discussion, captain, is getting us exactly no-where."

"Aye."

"Well, I think these will be our last words on this trip."

"Good."

Abner Smith stood staring at the slammed door for a long time. There was no doubt about her anger. But, he suspected, it was more than her concern over that Chinese glad-ass that had done it. Ab sighed.

He was turning away when Pooch came down the ladder.

"There's land not more'n eight miles off the larboard bow. The damn look-out never even saw it till a little while ago."

"That'd be one of the Paracels. They're low."

The world was miraculously still. No *shush* of a wake sounded astern. The hollow flap of a sail was followed by the clitter-clatter of reefpoints.

"What's more," Pooch added, "there's three boats putting out towards us, and I don't like the looks of 'em at all."

Chapter Eleven

THEY WERE a junk and two lorchas. Propelled by sweeps across an unwrinkled sea in which the *Forest* stood becalmed, each was a picture. The smaller craft, with their sweating, pigtailed oarsmen, poked perkily ahead, scooting over the surface like waterbugs. The junk moved with more grandeur—a vessel out of a fairy-story book, with orange and green bow-eyes, a rickety gaudy superstructure, and spars that jutted this way and that. Many men manned the junk, and some of these waved swords, while some struck gongs or set off fireworks and yelled. On the high stern castle, in addition to the tillerman, there was a priest in yellow robes who threw gilt paper into a fire before a yellow clay image.

"All that's for Me-tsoo-poo, their goddess of the sea," said Abner.

"Shouldn't think she'd need any appeasing in weather like this!"

"I'm not so sure," Ab muttered. The air was taut. No breeze blew, and there wasn't as much as a catspaw to ripple the surface of the sea. Though immediately around the bark all was serenity, the sky to the east was as ominous, in a different way, as the approaching Orientals. I'm afraid they're up to something."

High on the forward deck was enthroned a personage

in saffron. Many attended him, and two—even though the sun hung low—held an enormous umbrella over his head. He wore a small, square, black silk cap, on top of which was a blue button.

"Mandarin, third class," said Abner, and Kok Soo, nearby, nodded.

Pooch asked, "Important?"

"Tolerably. Any mandarin is."

"Would a man like that play pirate for us, maybe?"

"A man like that might even decide to *be* a pirate, if he thought he could sink the evidence. Go below, mister, and fetch out my pistols and load 'em. Load the muskets too."

The manœuvres of the newcomers were wary. Twice, at a discreet distance, the boats circled the becalmed bark.

At last the junk, ponderous, yet handled with skill, took up a place directly under the *Forest*'s bows, where her sweeps held her still. The lorchas ranged a little behind her, one on each side. In each vessel, stationed along the gunnels, ignoring the clamour, quietly alert, hard-eyed men held knotted ropes to which iron hooks were tied.

The purpose was plain. The stern chaser, a swivel gun, had been seen, as had the carronades, and since the impotence of the latter could hardly have been divined from a distance, all were being treated with respect. Not one of them could be trained upon the Chinese boats so long as those boats stayed dead ahead of the *Forest*.

There must have been at least three hundred men from the islands. Aboard the bark were seventeen—and two women. Yet the odds were not as great as figures might make them appear. There were factors that favoured the *Forest*.

There was the weather. A dead calm near the Paracels right in the middle of the north-east monsoon season was freakish; it could not last long. A storm was coming, and time counted. In another two hours it would be dark. Whatever was to be done must be done quickly.

The men from the islands were not sure of themselves. This foreign devil looked altogether too meek. Would anybody who commanded only a few men and three guns venture so close to the reefs? Where were his sailors? Would anybody who was not confident of his own strength await so calmly the approach of coasters? For everything aboard the bark was quiet. Abner had seen to that. The bos'n and his mates did not move. The Lascars were all below.

The newcomers hesitated.

This was as Abner wanted it. Let them worry. Bluff was an old Yankee game, and at this moment anyway it was the only game he *could* play.

At first sight of the visitors he had ordered that the swivel gun be loaded, but now nobody manned that weapon. With it Abner might have holed and conceivably even sunk one of the three vessels as they circled the bark. But what good would that do? The others were sure to get away, to return after dark with a swarm of boats. Besides, how did he know that these men were pirates and not port officials? The line between the two could be all but indistinguishable. Maybe they were making this cautious, circuitous approach simply because they feared that *he* was a pirate? In these waters nobody trusted anybody else.

So he waited, motionless.

Some time passed; and this was all to the good, from Abner's point of view.

On the junk there was much anxious conference. On the bark everything was still.

The sun, turgid, obese, was a strident red as it slid towards the horizon. The surface of the sea was silken.

Abner lounged against the bow. Like the mandarin he was smoking; but Abner smoked a cigar, while the Chinese puffed indolently at a porcelain-and-silver pipe all of three feet long. On the right and left of the mandarin men in long grass-green robes and conical rattan hats bound down with red silk cord assiduously fanned him.

Suddenly Ab looked aft. The thought had come to him that Anne Mackenzie, hearing the fire-crackers, the gongs, and the shouting, might leave her precious charge long enough to venture out for a look. It would be well to warn her against this. He looked around for somebody to send to her, but near him was only Kok Soo, whom he wished to keep there as an interpreter.

At this moment Kok Soo spoke up. "He says his ex-cellency will consent to come aboard and receive the ad-u-la-tion of the foreign devil."

A man who stood before the arm-chaired mandarin, seemingly some sort of secretary, had been doing a great deal of shouting; but until now Abner had paid no atten-tion.

"His excellency of what?"

"Namoo."

"Never heard of it."

Kok Soo shrugged.

"Did you?"

Kok Soo shook his head.

"Probably some reef that was created a port by imperial decree in order to give somebody's third cousin a chance to get a bite out of the wreckers' profits there."

Kok Soo nodded.

"Well, tell him to come ahead," said Abner. "Provided he doesn't bring anybody with him."

For all his air of indifference, Ab was very worried. Besides the men with the ropes and hooks there were other men who held round black tin balls, each about the size of a man's head, to which fuses had been attached. That was a bad sign. They could hurl those stench bombs or smoke bombs, following them with the grappling hooks, and then swarm aboard the bark in overwhelming numbers through the man-made murk. And they would do so, Ab figured, except that they were afraid they might be met by well-armed forces just now hidden below deck.

If they did attack, that would mean the end of the *Forest of Arden*. The pirates of the Paracels were not such fools as to leave traces. When vessels on this run disappeared, they disappeared entirely.

Darkness was coming soon. So was that storm. But— soon enough?

There was a great deal of shouting. Kok Soo reported that the mandarin insisted upon his customary attendants.

"Dig-ni-ty," Kok Soo explained with care.

Ab nodded. He was about to start to haggle when a new thought came to him and he waved a careless hand. They could see him from the junk, a fact of which he was intensely aware.

"All right. Let him bring as many as he pleases. And tell the cook to make tea."

The mandarin came gingerly over the planks, stepping with care. He had long stringy black moustaches and black, almost humorous old-monkey eyes. There was a dragon in silver and gold thread on his chest, a similar one on his back. His feet were not in sight. At no point was he commonplace or drab, but perhaps the most distinctive things about him were his hands. He carried a fingering-piece made of Mogaung green jadeite carved in the likeness of K'wan Yin, the goddess of mercy, and he never ceased to stir this in his long, pale, almost transparent hands, just as he never ceased to smile. He was fragile, and probably venomous. He had beautiful manners. Though he ruled a maritime province, scarcely more than a raft of rock, it was clear to Ab that this man was ill at ease on the water. Perhaps he had a weak stomach? Certainly he was frail, and his temples were touched with a slightly greenish hue that suggested queasiness. Several times as he came over the planks he glanced nervously towards the east, where clouds thickened. Abner wondered if he was the kind of man—he had met them like that—who could get sick at the very thought of a storm. Clearly it was not his custom to come out and greet every vessel that approached his stronghold. Abner should have felt flattered, he supposed. He didn't; he only felt uneasy. But he continued to smoke his cigar.

The Lord of Namoo was properly preceded and followed, and on deck all but surrounded, by a secretary; an umbrella bearer; four men in green, two of them holding fans, one holding a spittoon, while the fourth carried his excellency's back-scratcher; and four tall, muscle-knotty Chinese with swords. The swords were real ones, not ceremonial pieces.

It was the last group that most interested Abner Smith, and especially its leader, a swart, short, squat man with a

F

tremendous neck, and arms so long that his gorilla-like hands dangled almost to the knee. This man was utterly bald—there was not even a fringe of fuzz on his neck— and he wore huge golden crescent earrings that swung back and forth. Here seemed a person of great potential power, though presently no more than captain of body-guards at an out-of-the-way court. He listened little, doubt-less because he knew that most of what would be said would mean nothing; but his eyes were active.

" What's that man's name? " Abner whispered to Kok Soo, who had been fraternizing diffidently with the soldiers.

" Shap'ngtzai."

" Again? "

" Shap'ngtzai," the bos'n whispered. " They say he is a great fighter."

" I can believe it."

Of all the mandarin's immediate attendants this Shap'-ngtzai alone did not double up when his master spoke to him. In fact, his manner, if not actually insubordinate, was cold. Not only did he refuse to grovel but he remained patently unimpressed with the mandarin's rank, and there were times when he regarded his aristocratic, over-civilized master with contempt and, Abner estimated, with hatred. Yet Shap'ngtzai did not spend much time studying the man he guarded. His eyes were busy elsewhere. They lit upon the belaying-pin rack, in which there were no belay-ing-pins. Possibly Shap'ngtzai concluded from this that the pins were clutched in the hands of sailors who awaited a signal to charge out into the open. Abner could hope so, anyway; it was in this hope that he had caused the pins to be hidden. Shap'ngtzai noted too, with great interest, as

Abner could see, that the touch-holes of the carronades had been smashed.

If the visitors were wondering how many men were hidden below they must have been disappointed when Abner halted them in the waist.

That this official was despot only of a pile of rocks made for not less but rather more reason to observe all formalities in his presence. The farther away the exile, the fussier he could be.

Abner, then, bowed. He implored forgiveness from the great and gracious lord, explaining that nowhere else but here in the waist of his all-unworthy ship was any proper conference convenient.

Kok Soo interpreted this gruffly, but Abner's manner counted.

Ab told Pooch to bring up the chair from their cabin—the only chair on the ship—and place it facing south, the direction of happy augury. He begged the mandarin to seat himself. He clapped his hands and called for tea. It was good tea too, a smoky, heavy souchong.

Ordinarily there would be at least one hour of this before any mention was made of business. The mandarin, however, had not forgotten that lowering sky. He drew from his sleeve a red document, which he passed to the secretary, who read it aloud.

"True copy of Imperial Edict dated Tao-Kuang, 17th year, 6th moon, 4th sun. As the port of Canton is the only one at which the Outer Barbarians are permitted to trade, on no account can they be allowed to wander and visit other places in the Middle Kingdom. His Majesty, however, being ever desirous that his compassion be made manifest even to the least deserving, cannot deny to such as are in distress from lack of food through adverse seas and currents the necessary means of continuing their voyage. When supplied, these must not linger but put to sea again immediately. Tremble, intensely tremble! Respect this!"

Abner bowed again; whereupon the mandarin, with a most unoriental abruptness, asked him how much opium he had.

Abner told him. But Abner raised a finger for attention, and signalled to the tindals, who opened the Number 2 Hatch and brought up one of the chests.

A good wine, the saying goes, needs no bush. This stuff, this ineffable Malwa, called for no touting on the part of Captain Smith, who kept his peace, permitting the poppy product to speak for itself.

The mandarin had been disciplined to eschew all show of emotion—he would have made a crack poker player, Ab reflected—but even he could not resist a catch of the breath, a faint but perceptible flare of his old eyes when he looked at the opened chest. He put aside the fingering-piece and lifted a ball. He peeled off the leaves. He raised the muck to his nose. He sniffed and closed his eyes in well-bred ecstasy.

There was a rumble from the east, and a small sudden gust of wind rattled the reef-points.

From the other direction, where the sun was low, they could hear the muffled thunder of a reef, presumably part of the island from which these men had come. Their vessels were drifting towards it.

The mandarin opened his eyes. A curious film came over them, as though only his will kept them from glittering. He was no longer looking at the opium he held, but at something over Abner's left shoulder.

They were all looking that way.

Ab turned.

On the after deck stood the " Manchu princess " Shen Ti. Poised on the balls of her feet, she had the grace of a bird that has just alighted and at any instant may take off again. Her chin was high. Her neck was bare, and it could have been carved of ivory, as her hair could have been lacquered onto the exquisite head.

After the first gasp from the islanders there was a stunned silence, but the men's eyes glittered lustfully, and their lips were working, their tongues going back and forth, while each gripped with a compulsive tightness whatever it was that he held—fan, cuspidor, scroll, sword.

No doubt the whore knew this. No doubt those stares smote her as applause smites the ears of an actress. Statuesque, encarnadined by the setting sun, she did not stir.

She had that moment, her moment, and it was a memorable one. Then Anne Mackenzie came up through the hatch and went to her and with an arm around her led her back to the cabin.

All this took no more than a minute. The thunder sounded again, not so far away this time, and the mandarin was himself again; yet when he returned to the matter at hand he was, all things considered, curt. It hardly mattered to Ab. All he wanted now was to get rid of the opium at a fair price—and get rid of the visitors at the same time.

It was a touch-and-go matter. These boarders, had they been sure of themselves, would gladly have taken the cargo by force—together with the ship, not to mention the lives of all aboard. A mis-step here might provoke a fight; and a fight could end only one way.

The greenness at the mandarin's temples had spread to his cheeks under his eyes; his upper lip gleamed with sweat, and, for all his formalism, there was agony in his eyes. He was weakening fast, on the verge of collapse. The captain of the guard was the one to watch. Shap'-ngtzai, Abner believed, would have roamed the deck, snooping, had not his ceremonious duties kept him stationed near his master. For one thing, he must have been wondering why the forecastle hatch was shut.

Another gust of wind made the reef-points patter, the canvas flap. The deck gently rose and fell. And now the mandarin, becoming desperate, cast custom aside and all but blurted his terms.

Abner made a rapid mental calculation—the offer had been stated in taels of silver—and came up with a figure of slightly more than nineteen hundred dollars a chest for the whole cargo. This was as good a price as he could have hoped to get in port. Moreover, though there would have to be a gift from seller to buyer, the time-honoured " squeeze ", without which such a transaction would be unthinkable, Abner would have no other expense—no extra bribes, no unloading fee, not even a wharfage or an anchorage charge. The exchange could be effected right at sea, in the lee of one of the nearby islands after the storm had passed; and then the *Forest* could proceed to Canton with half a million dollars worth of silver with which to buy cargo for the run home—nankeens and tea, perhaps, and some shalloons, blue gurrah, patchouli, ostrich feathers, rice. Even if Andy Thompson took command again at Singapore, there was no doubt that Abner, having handled a deal like that, would be given a ship of his own.

He kept asking himself: Where's the trick? Where is the joker?

Not the least curious feature of this curious scene was the fact that the bargaining attitudes were the reverse of the usual. It was the Oriental who sought to push the deal through, while the white man, the Occidental, hesitated, picked flaws, and suggested another cup of tea.

The mandarin of course was preparing to violate one of the Emperor's own edicts; but he was a long way from Peking. He had the silver. He knew the value of Malwa, and knew too how seldom such stuff could be found in these parts. He must have had a market in mind. He must have sniffed a giddy profit, one that would permit him to buy his way back into the Imperial court.

Even so—where was the joker?

Abner paused for a fleet instant. He glanced west to where the red sun all but tagged the horizon, to where the reef creamed. He glanced east, and saw the swift-coming squall. He bowed. He declared that the mandarin's terms were accepted.

The mandarin bowed.

Then, through Kok Soo, Abner asked that he be permitted to offer his excellency some manner of small gift in order to show his gratitude for the honour that had been paid him. The mandarin gravely replied that he would consent to such a procedure. Abner asked if his excellency would exhibit the great kindness and condescension to make known what manner of gift might be acceptable to him.

The mandarin did.

Captain Smith bowed. He begged to be excused from his excellency's august presence for a few short minutes, and without waiting for an answer he turned on his heel and went aft.

"Who is it?" Anne Mackenzie called, when he knocked on the door of her cabin.

"Open up. That's a command."

A moment—and then she stood there defiant, her back a ramrod.

"Captain, I thought I made it clear that——"

"Shut up. This won't wait."

"If it's your purpose to condemn me for letting Shen Ti run out on deck like that, all I can say is that I'm sorry."

"So am I," Ab said with much feeling. "Now listen——"

He told her about the bargaining, the settlement, the squeeze. He was brief, but emphatic. She listened well.

"And what did he ask for?"

Abner looked at her. "Can't you guess?"

Just for a moment it would seem that she couldn't. Then she whirled around and threw her arms around Shen Ti.

"No! They can't take her! You mustn't let them!"

"Ma'am, control yourself. I am not going to steal your Chink. All I came for was to ask you not to let her get loose again like that."

"Oh, I'll be careful. I will, captain. And—thank you."

"I am going back now to tell the mandarin that he can't have the woman he asked for."

There were tears in her eyes as she raised her head. "Thank you," she whispered. "I—I owe you an apology. Here——"

She stretched up on tiptoe and kissed him.

It was a short kiss, but there was nothing perfunctory

about it. It was full, soft, warm. Then she ran back
into the cabin and closed the door.

Abner stood a moment in the semi-darkness of the
passageway. He had enjoyed that kiss. But he could not
help wondering whether he had deserved it.

Because it was not Shen Ti the mandarin had asked for.
It was Anne Mackenzie.

Chapter Twelve

WHEN HE came up on deck Abner quickly noted
three things:

First: The storm was nearer now, alarmingly near.

Second: The mandarin was about to be sick.

Third: Shap'ngtzai was trying to open the forecastle
hatch.

Each one of these things was of importance, but it was on
the third one that Ab acted. If the bald-headed captain of
bodyguards had a look down there and saw scarcely more
than a dozen Lascars armed with no more than knives, he
might call upon his men to take over the bark. Ab believed
that it had been Shap'ngtzai's inclination to do that from
the beginning, for he was obviously a man of action, not
a courtier, and he must have been impatient with all this
bowing and scraping, all this palavering and tea-drinking.
He had taken advantage of his master's nausea and Abner's
absence to climb to the forward deck, and now he was
about to call Abner's bluff.

There was nothing behind that bluff.

Abner did not take the ladder but literally leaped into the waist. He paid no heed to the mandarin, who, pale as death, rocked in his chair. There was, as Ab passed, a shocked, indignant twittering among the attendants at this breach of etiquette.

Abner scrambled up to the forward deck. Shap'ngtzai was on his knees trying to force open the hatch. Abner went to his own knees, confronting him, and grasped both his wrists.

"You do that," Ab said, speaking in a low voice right into the soldier's face, "and I'll throw you overboard."

The Chinese, of course, could not understand a word of this. But he could understand the tone of voice; he could understand the eyes, the strong hands.

Shap'ngtzai was immensely strong, and could have torn himself free of Abner as a bear might fling off a terrier. He had many men stationed within call. And Abner's insistence that there be no look into the forecastle was itself a confession of weakness.

Abner could read the shrewd understanding in the soldier's face during the split-second while they knelt, glaring at one another.

Abner often had wondered, after three visits to the Orient, why folks back home habitually designated all Chinese as "inscrutable". They were the most expressive race in the world, he thought. It was because they wept so easily that they made it a rule to control themselves at funerals by the only means at their command—laughter. Again, it was because they laughed so readily that, knowing this, they kept a grip on themselves on ordinary occasions by an extraordinary show of solemnity, which deceived nobody who knew them. If they were indeed "impassive" it was only because they dared not let themselves be otherwise. It was the Chinese who produced the word "face". Except for those who, like the mandarin, had trained themselves through long and arduous years to keep a straight countenance, they were absurdly easy to read.

The thoughts of Shap'ngtzai here, for example, were as clear as though they had been printed in large block letters on a sign. He was concerned about the storm, which would strike soon. Shap'ngtzai may or may not have been a sailing man, but he was an islander. He was at all times aware of the weather. By trying to prevent him from opening the forecastle hatch, by putting hands on him, Abner had given him an excuse to fight, if he thought a fight advisable. It was not a matter of personal courage. It was a matter of time.

Shap'ngtzai's own fighting experience, no doubt, had been of the hit-and-run variety. He was used to quick victories. Yet he must have known that white men were singularly stubborn in battle and had been seen to refuse to retreat long after it became clear that they'd been whipped. Specifically, if Shap'ngtzai called for a conflict here and now, he and his associates might find themselves, in the end, cut off from their companions. For the storm would be violent. Already the lorchas and junk, not dependent on canvas but propelled by sweeps, were edging away. Soon they'd make a dash for shore. They were never built, those vessels, to ride out a hurricane; nor would the men in them care to do so while it still remained possible to reach the shelter of a lagoon. Trapped in a vessel different from any in which they had ever sailed, a vessel they did not know how to handle, and having just slaughtered all such men as *could* handle it, Shap'ngtzai and his associates might perish in the storm.

There was another consideration, strong even though secondary. In the course of a battle it was possible, even probable, that the small weak mandarin, trapped in the waist, would be killed. That Shap'ngtzai hated his master Abner believed. But habit and training were powerful factors; and Shap'ngtzai, a soldier, knew his duty, which was to protect that spindly blue-blood. This was made clear once again when the mandarin, at this crucial moment, called aloud for his captain.

The Chinese warrior hesitated only a moment. Then he rose, and Abner released him. The mandarin called again; and again over Shap'ngtzai's eyes there passed a wave of hatred. Yet he would go. He'd answer that call, a bleat now.

Suddenly he grinned at Abner, and Ab grinned back. It was a little like making friends with a grizzly bear, but these two strong men understood one another. Language isn't everything.

Shap'ngtzai returned to the waist, Ab following. The mandarin was truly sick now, using a cuspidor held by an attendant. Though he couldn't speak to answer, he was being addressed, respectfully but urgently by a personage Abner took to be the skipper of one of the Chinese vessels, clearly a seafaring man anyway. The attendant, too, looked anxious, straining as they apprehensively watched the sky. Everybody was eager to leave.

Abner seized this moment to propose—formally through Kok Soo, and in the most flowery language he could concoct—that they have another cup of tea.

Such a request called for an answer. It could not be ignored. The mandarin raised his head. Though vomit dribbled from the corners of his mouth, he managed somehow to smile. He started to speak—he tried to point to the junk—and fainted dead away.

After that it was a rush. Fearful both for the health of their lord and the safety of their own skins, the visitors, carrying the limp mandarin, could not get away fast enough. Within a few minutes there wasn't a Chinese aboard *Forest of Arden*, excepting Kok Soo and his two tindals, who were opening the forecastle hatch and shouting for all hands to come up on deck.

Moments later, with the decisiveness of a slammed door, the storm came.

Chapter Thirteen

THE BARK was ready for it. Paradoxically, the *Firefly*'s attack had strengthened *Forest of Arden*, at least as far as meeting a high blow was concerned. Fresh canvas had been brought out, and every replacement checked, every line tightened. There was still a great deal of work to be done on *Forest* before she'd be her usual speedy self again; but for storm purposes, for an immediate emergency, she was as sound as ever.

The Lascars too were ready for it. The opium fumes had been dissipated; the men's heads were clear again. True, they were tired, for Pooch and Abner had worked them mercilessly getting the damage repaired. But much as they might hate their officers, they had sense enough to see now that their lives depended upon working—and work they did.

For a few minutes after the first shock there was some danger of collision. The Chinese vessels, though swift, had only begun to pull away from the *Forest*; but when last seen—when they were blotted from sight by rain— they were making frantic speed for the islands. No doubt their skippers knew those islands and could move in and out of them as a man knows his own bedroom and even in darkness can move among the pieces of furniture there. No doubt those skippers knew every bay, cove, and lagoon, every reef, whether exposed or submerged, every protecting arm of land, shoal, mushroom, niggerhead—and knew them in all-obliterating rain and spume, by ear, by feel, rather than sight. Understandably, then, the Chinese vessels headed for land. With their sweeps, their ample freeboard, and wide rudders, they were highly manœuvrable.

But for the *Forest of Arden* there could be no cover. Ab Smith's hope lay in riding it out. At all costs he must keep away from those islands.

The sea, after being so calm, began to shiver and shake, and its surface consisted now of millions of silvery speartips. It was as though the land beneath the water, the very bottom itself, was being agitated, a sub-aqueous earthquake. The small, terse waves spat as they rose, each with the malice of an uprearing viper; but this sound was soon swamped in the thunder of rain.

When the rain came it took over the whole world. Had this been noon they still could not have seen more than a few feet in any direction. There was wind now, and it was rising, though it was not yet ready to strip the tops off the waves and send them spewing and whistling across *Forest*'s deck; but the drops were so large that they appeared to bounce off the bark, then break up so that their shattered fragments formed a mist that prickled the skin while it shut off the sight as a fog would have done.

When it was that the rain stopped nobody knew. Nor did anybody care. It was much the same, except that after a while they came to realize that the water that stung their hands and faces was from off the sea, not from out of the sky, for it was salty, not fresh. This made no practical difference.

The wind was still rising, a horrid howl.

The seas were not running free, as they would have in an ordinary blow. There was no accounting for them. They leaped and jostled together crazily, higher and higher. They hissed as they rose in impotent rage, as if striving to smite the sky, and they hissed when they fell back to gather strength for another reach. Though the *Forest* lurched and pitched from the side-thrust of them, it was not often, there in the beginning of the blow, that one of these seas crashed across her deck—at least in the form of solid water, what sailors call "green water". For all this fact, the scuppers were cataracts, so thick was the spray.

Abner frowned in annoyance when the after hatch was opened and Anne Mackenzie came out. What did she want on deck at a time like this? He had started towards her and was about to order her back below when she saw him and smiled at him.

It was a good full smile, no mere smirk; and in view of

their recent relations, in view of their predicament, it felt
very good to Abner. It warmed him. Forgetting himself,
he grinned at her.

"I'll be below," she shouted, her face not four inches
from his.

"Good," he shouted back. "Is *she* all right?"

"I think she's frightened. But she can move."

"Good. She may have to."

Anne stood with feet spread wide apart, her left hand
clinging to a stay, her right arm helping her to hold her
balance as though she were an acrobat walking a tight-
rope.

One of the lines that ran to the sea-anchor let loose at
this instant, and it took with it, in addition to a snubbing
post, almost half the taffrail. Also, the grinding crash badly
loosened the lines that lashed the Moses boat, brought
inboard before the blow. That craft rocked frantically,
squealing as though in pain. The two helmsmen looked
back at it, badly frightened. Pooch Palmer ran to it, as
did Abner; but there was no holding it.

"Pitch it over," Ab yelled.

They slashed the lines, then shoved the thing with their
feet, holding to one another for fear of being swept away
with it. The Moses, a trim white little boat that had taken
Abner ashore in many an exotic port, a well-behaved good-
looking boat, was snapped off the stern and vanished in a
lathered wake.

The longboat still was secure. Not that it meant anything. In weather like this they could never launch a boat
anyway. If the *Forest of Arden* went down they would go
down with it. But it made the helmsmen feel easier.

Ab returned to the girl. "I'll close the hatch after you,"

he shouted. "You won't get trapped. But I don't want it left open, even an inch."

"All right!"

She started away, while he watched her; but she turned back. She came close to him again.

"I'll pray for us," she shouted.

"Good," he shouted. "We're going to need every bit of help we can get!"

He saw her safely into the companionway, and saw that the hatch was fastened behind her before he started to crack out a spare sea-anchor.

The storm that night was sheer raving madness, following no pattern. A true typhoon would have given them some hours, if not days, of drenching, sweeping rain; and then it would have settled down to blow with terrific force, and the fight would be on. But you'd know where you stood—or floated. You would know *how* to fight. True, its centre might pass over you, and then you would find that it was blowing, and just as hard, from the opposite direction, which would call for some marvellously quick handling. But you could be prepared for that.

The storm that night off the Paracels obeyed no rules whatever. Abner did not know at any given time which way they were headed, much less how near to the reefs they might be. The bark was buffeted like an eggshell.

His first hope was that this was some sort of freak squall that would soon pass. But it kept on, and on.

There was no profit in looking at the compass, which spun back and forth so fast that the figures could not be read. The best he could do was to try to keep *Forest* faced up into it—wherever it was. He could see nothing in that

G

smother of foam, any more than the helmsman could. He took half the wheel a couple of times himself, as Pooch did. It was no use. They weren't a bit better than the scared Lascars.

He had three main problems, aside from the very great problem of simply staying afloat: to keep the ship headed into the weather, to be sure that the hatches were tight, and to stay clear of that shore.

For way he depended entirely upon storm jibs, with a second suit near at hand. He'd had storm topsails in readiness too, but he did not dare to send anybody aloft to rig them. Bluntly, he would not have ventured up there himself, and so he would not command anybody else to do it. Pooch might have taken the risk, but Abner could not spare his mate, who might be carried away.

They had plenty of storm canvas, thank God, but they had plenty of use for it too. After the first sea-anchor was lost and they had set out the second, Abner ordered two more to be jury-made from the spare suit of storm topsails; but this was not a job that could be done with speed in such conditions.

Of the hatches he was tolerably sure. *Forest of Arden* was well built, and Abner as first mate and as skipper always had been fussy about hatches. Still, the seas were higher now, and sometimes one of them slashed across the waist, hundreds of tons of angry water. If ever a hatch was torn off there would be no chance to patch it: the bark would be flooded in a matter of minutes, perhaps even seconds, and they'd capsize or sink. Every time he passed a hatch, staggering, clinging to one of the knotted storm lines he had caused to be rigged fore-and-aft, he studied it anxiously.

And—where was land? This was the greatest dread. When the storm hit them they had been about eight miles from the low-lying shore. Where were they now? He didn't know. They must be drifting, but he had no way of learning the direction of that drift. They might drive aground, or have their bottom ripped out, at any moment.

To listen for breakers in such a blow seemed a bit absurd. Yet he did so, morbidly. He told one of Kok Soo's tindals, a man noted for his acute hearing, to encircle the ship constantly, with his ears cocked. Not satisfied with this, or it could have been plain nervousness, Abner began to work his own way around . . . and around . . . lurching, reeling, grasping this line, that spar, anything that came to hand—never venturing to trust himself without a grip—soaked, bruised, stumbling, slipping—forward along the larboard rail, aft along the starboard rail, across the poop, forward along the larboard rail again—checking damage as he went, shouting encouragement to the hands —and all the while hoping that he would never hear breakers.

It was not he who heard them first, after all. It was the tindal.

Abner was on the poop, supervising the launching of the third sea-anchor, a flimsy, hastily constructed affair, the second having been carried away, when the tindal tugged at his elbow, making wild motions. The man couldn't talk English, but it was clear what he meant. He was pointing forward. Ab nodded, almost casually, and followed him.

Hand over hand, struggling, gasping, they made it.

The *Forest* was rolling wide at this time but not pitching much, and they were able to brace themselves against the capstan, far forward, without much danger of being washed overboard.

It was breakers, all right. They were dead ahead, as far as Abner could figure, and startlingly near. Their throaty rumble came clear and menacing underneath the wind's insane yowl.

Abner sent the tindal away. The man would know what to do: he'd take the order from Abner's face—tell all hands to stand by for a jump.

There wasn't anything else. The wind was in one of its rare moods of steadiness, driving them straight towards the breakers' roar, that was growing louder every moment.

Abner heaved himself up to the rail and clung to it, staring ahead of the vessel with eyes that could not see. The darkness told him nothing, as his compass too, that miserable man-made device, had told him nothing at all. Truly this was the way it always had been, blind, had he but admitted it. This was the way it was with every man. Abner, the captain of his own ship, the master of his own fate? Nonsense. He was utterly helpless, spellbound, standing there waiting to be dashed to pieces on rocks he couldn't even see.

He drew a deep breath. He turned, and ran aft.

This time he really did run. He didn't lunge from place to place, from handgrip to handgrip.

There was no need to give the alarm. The tindal had already done so. Moreover, by the time Abner reached the poop the sound of breakers had been heard by everybody there.

The crew were quiet, and he was sorry now that he had docked them half their pay—pay they'd never get anyway.

Pooch Palmer, who was helping at the helm, knew as well as Ab what was coming.

Abner checked the sea-anchor, a flimsy affair. If it held, they would drive straight ahead into the reef or solid shore. If it was indeed a reef, there was a thousand-to-one chance that they'd slip through a break in it. However, if this sea-anchor carried away as the others had done, they would swing sideways, either broaching-to or else smashing beam-wise against the rocks.

He went to the after hatch and worked it open.

"Come up, Anne," he shouted. And added to himself: "Come up and die."

Chapter Fourteen

IT MIGHT have been the mountains of the moon, much truncated; or some wilderness that God had forgotten to finish; or again, in Pooch Palmer's phrase, Hell with the fires out.

Yet it was paradise, that pearl morning, to those on the deck of the *Forest of Arden*.

As soon as there was light enough, Abner got out the glass and made a long slow-sweeping study of the land that surrounded them. What he saw was mostly rocks—gaunt, grey-and-brown, Druidical, Stonehengy slabs that jutted this way and that, drab, dour, dreary. Some, near the shore, were covered with slime that glistened in the light of the rising sun. Others looked parched, flinty.

There were no trees, and the only vegetation was a dry, brittle, juiceless grass, of no particular colour, that grew in clumps. It was the bleakest conceivable landscape—or combination landscape and seascape, rather, for there was a great deal of water among these strips and blobs of land, and it was sometimes difficult to tell where one started and the other left off.

The bark floated free, almost listlessly, as though tired, in the middle of a broad lagoon. Elsewhere, at places where the shore was not protected as it was here by out-reaching reefs, surfs slammed sullenly against the rocks, sometimes mounting as a geyser's column through an unseen blowhole, wavering, breaking into millions of iridescent drops. There was no movement save the languid, lolling glide of the gulls overhead.

Far to eastward, where the land mass was more con-sistent, not being so striated with arms of the sea, Abner could make out the roofs of huts. This was the only sign of humanity outside of the bark itself, and it was not a cheering sign. No smoke rose from any of the huts, which might have made up an abandoned fishing village. Aside from the gulls there were no living creatures in sight. Aside from the surf there was no sound.

If it came to that, the scene aboard the *Forest of Arden* itself could scarcely be called animated. Had it not been for Abner and his mate and Miss Anne Mackenzie, the only ones upright, the vessel the dawn revealed might have been thought a plague ship. Water no longer swished across the deck and tumbled in the scuppers; wind no longer screeched through the rigging; and the bark's buffeted timbers were silent at last. Once they had fumbled through that narrow pass in the reef to attain the relative tranquillity of this lagoon—though at that time the wind still was high—Abner had ordered a hook let go. And once he was sure that this hook did not drag, he had dismissed all hands. Down they'd dropped, right where they were, exhausted, stupefied with fatigue. They spent no time seeking out their bunks in the forecastle, which probably was flooded anyway.

Now the jibs hung limp. The drying stays and shrouds were slack. Behind the trio on the poop deck the wheel rocked a little, a lazy motion, while behind that the two men who had last held it snored unceasingly. Near the skylight Shen Ti was motionless, sitting on her heels, her head bowed forward. She had wept herself to sleep, exhausted by her fears as the others had been by their exertions. All over the waist and the forward deck, as though strewn there by a giant's hand, Lascars and Chinese alike sprawled this way and that. None of them so much as twitched or moaned.

In the lagoon, opalescent now, there was not a ripple, and no fish jumped there.

Abner handed the glass to his passenger. "Have a peek? It's not very promising."

She took it without looking up, though she murmured thanks. They were both embarrassed. Short hours ago, braced against what remained of the taffrail, they had waited side by side for death to strike; and his arm had been around her. Everything had been done that could be done. It only remained to wait for the bark to strike. They were determined to jump, and he had fetched an oar from the longboat for her to hang on to—if she could.

Not only did they cling to one another; they had kissed repeatedly. And those were long, hard impassioned kisses.

Each thought, and knew that the other thought, of the time that they had wasted—until it was too late.

It had been a wonderful five minutes—a five minutes well worth all the rest of their lives put together.

Then—the hole in the reef.

It was not a sound that they heard so suddenly—and all but miraculously in the midst of that tumult—but rather an absence of sound, a void in the raging yammer of breakers.

With a whoop Abner had seized the wheel, shoving the helmsmen aside. He could see nothing. He literally steered by ear. It had taken all his strength and all his skill as well to hold the vessel away from the reef a little longer, to claw off that death-studded shore.

They watched him, fascinated. There was nothing else that anybody could do. It was a matter of holding the bark head on until the pass, if there was a pass, was reached and entered. Abner's ears might tell him where that was. They could not tell him whether it was straight enough to take the *Forest of Arden*—or wide enough—or deep enough.

The sea-anchor, their third, had held. Otherwise they would have swung broadside to the reef and been smashed to splinters. Even head-on they had made it with no more than a few feet of clearance.

Then for a brief time the whole world appeared to be coming apart while Abner fought the wheel. Great jagged rocks, doused in a smother of foam, loomed on either side, while ahead, after a while, they could glimpse the lagoon, comparatively tranquil.

Somehow, Abner still hanging on, they had stumbled to safety, and dropped the hook. And a little later the wind had fallen, and the dawn had come, painting everything with pastels.

Sunset is always dramatic, even when murky. Sunrise is always an anticlimax. Though glad enough to find themselves alive, Anne and Abner somehow felt let down. And they did not like to look at one another.

Even when she was staring through the glass, Abner was reluctant to look at her, fearing that Pooch would notice his expression. Abner knew that he was in love, and that to battle this emotion, now that they'd gone so far, would be silly and a waste of strength. But he also knew that this was no time to be thinking about love. He shook himself angrily, impatiently. He turned sternwards to study the pass in the reef, now that there was enough light.

It was amazingly narrow. He marvelled that they had squeezed through. He wondered if they would be able to get out again. Though he sagged with weariness and all his muscles ached, he made his plans.

As soon as they had rested, he and Pooch Palmer would go over every inch of the hull from the inside, then strip and go over everything from the outside as well. They had certainly scraped when they came through that pass— twice Abner had distinctly felt it, deep down as though along the keel itself—and something might be sprung. If the vessel needed careening he reckoned that this would be as good a place as any for the job.

After that he would have out the longboat and make an elaborate series of soundings all back and forth across the lagoon and then through the pass itself. Here was where they might run into trouble. High seas and a high wind had pushed them into the lagoon—with inches of bottom to spare, if that much. They could count on no such assistance getting out. They might have to jettison some or even all of their cargo, a melancholy prospect.

" Abner——"

He turned.

" Aye? "

While he had been gazing at the pass his mate had taken the glass from Anne Mackenzie. Now Pooch passed this to Abner. He motioned towards the cluster of huts.

" Over there——"

The light was better now, for it was fully day. Abner raised the glass.

A column of men was approaching the lagoon from the direction of the huts. They were soldiers all right, for they marched in military fashion and the rising sun glinted against bits of metal—a spear tip, a sword hilt, the muzzle of a fowling piece. At their head stalked a figure unmistakable even at this distance, with his huge, round, completely bald head shining in the sun—Shap'ngtzai.

Abner lowered the glass.

" Get out the rifles."

Chapter Fifteen

"TRUST IN God," Cromwell told his troops, "but keep your powder dry."

It was a sentiment Abner Smith would have endorsed. In the gun locker in his own cabin he had an ample supply of good corned powder, besides two large chunks of lead, also a mould, scales, rods, wads, a rammer, a wiper, and all the rest of it—enough to take care of the ship's small arms: three rifles and four pistols. The swivel gun, a brass six-pounder, was another matter. It used what was known as "semi-fixed" ammunition, each ball being belted to a wad, while the powder, separate, was done up in measured charges inside of woollen bags, the whole being rammed in together. They also had some grape, and this too came in woollen bags. Because unburned bits of the wool sometimes foiled the rifling, it was necessary, in order to keep the gun firing true, to have on hand always an armoury of accessories—wormer, sponge, handspikes, a linstock of course, with extra fuses, and priming powder, a rammer, a cat, a scraper, and sundry other tools. These had been brought topside when the three Chinese boats appeared, and were now conveniently stored in a spare sail closet. Abner began getting them out while Pooch went below for the small arms.

The gun had been loaded, too, at the appearance of the mandarin's fleet, and it remained loaded.

Anne Mackenzie was watching him. "I've often wondered how those things work," she said. "Does it make much noise?"

"Tolerable."

He untaped the touch-hole, thrust his primer into it, and twisted this a few times. He inserted a friction stick. He lighted the match of his linstock.

"Are you going to shoot it off now?"

"Not likely." He took the tompion from the muzzle. "Even with this thing on, it's pretty sure to have got wet in the storm. But pulling the charge out is quite a job. I'd rather shoot it out—if it'll go off."

He glanced towards the approaching soldiers. Without the glass he could barely see them, and surely they weren't coming fast. He looked around the deck, at the sleeping, dead-seeming sailors. He had not awakened them. They'd earned their sleep, he reckoned, and he would let them have it. The soldiers still were far away, and there was no immediate alarm. He took his time.

It was a singularly peaceful scene. The lull before battle perhaps? Surf boomed rhythmically. Now and then a gull, wheeling gracefully overhead, gave forth a querulous caw.

Ab checked the recoil cables.

"How do you aim it?" she asked.

"By swinging it any way you want. It goes through two hundred and sixty degrees of a circle. Here, I'll show you——"

He pointed it at a neck of land a couple of hundred yards away. Beyond that was another lagoon. It was nowhere near the soldiers.

"With solid shot that would overcarry, but it happens to be loaded with grape."

"What's grape?"

"A whole lot of little balls instead of one big one."

He touched the linstock to the fuse, which began to splutter. Nothing else happened.

After a while Anne took her fingers out of her ears. "I'm disappointed," she said.

"They're tricky. Sometimes they—"

The gun went off.

Shen Ti, jolted awake, started to scream in terror. Several of the men sat up, mumbling questions. Others only twitched in their sleep. His arms full of weapons, Pooch came scrambling up the ladder.

"Are we being attacked?"

"Not yet."

Abner himself, though certainly startled, had turned his head in time to see where the shot landed. On that narrow peninsula chips of rock and spear-points of dirt leaped into the air.

"Good. It's laid right, too. We'll leave it that way."

He took up the glass again. The soldiers had halted, doubtless because they had heard the shot. Apparently the mandarin wasn't among them; at least Abner saw no umbrella.

He put down the glass and took the firearms from his mate. "Miss Mackenzie and I'll load these, mister. Now I want you to wake up a couple of hands and crack out the longboat and sound me that pass out there—every foot of it."

"You going to fight 'em off, Ab?"

"I don't know what I'm going to do, yet. Anyway, it's their move. Now get going."

Time was what he craved. It would take most of the day to get those soundings. It would take most of the following day to make an examination of the *Forest of Arden*. The Chinese and Lascars would be of no use there; the job must be done personally by Pooch and himself, checking one another. It was important to learn about the tides. It might prove advisable to shift their anchorage, and since there was no breeze this would call for towage by the longboat, a back-breaking task that in itself would occupy many hours.

The tide he figured roughly by having Pooch on his way

to the pass visit the rocky promontory that Ab had fired upon, which was the nearest land to the bark and at the same time the farthest land from the approaching army. There the mate drove into the sloping beach a series of stakes, to each of which had been tied a piece of bright-coloured cloth. Then, after Pooch had gone on to his lead-swinging duties, Abner at regular intervals of time would study these stakes through the glass and mark down their positions relative to the edge of the water. It was a crude system, but the best he could devise.

All this paper work, together with the routine of cleaning ship, irritated Anne. "What are you going to do about them?" And she would point to the Chinese soldiers, who, having halted for several hours, had taken up their march again and were about to occupy the beach.

"Depends on what they do. I told you, the next move is up to them. I'm not even sure whether we *can* move. That's what Pooch is trying to find out."

"But—aren't you even trying to *imagine* what they might do."

"Why, sure. I reckon they'll pitch camp over there and make what army men call a demonstration of strength—you know, wave their swords and all. Then they'll send out some high-muck-amuck who's all covered with gold tassel, and in the name of the mandarin he will demand that we land our mud. They'll announce that they are still getting the silver together, but we'll never see it. Then they'll declare us a wreck and seize the vessel."

"But we're not a wreck!"

"Of course not. We've still got all three of our sticks, and as far as I know nothing's been sprung."

"Isn't it contrary to international law to———"

"Let's forget about international law. There ain't no such animal out here."

"What if we resist?"

"Then they'll overwhelm us. Sooner or later they're bound to, as long as they don't care how many men they lose—and they won't. So they'll seize us and jail us. In fact, it's my bet that they would put us in jail even if we *didn't* resist. Then they'd say we tried to escape, and they'd kill us all. That is," he amended, looking the other way, "almost all of us."

He heard her swallow before she spoke again. "And what are you going to do when you get this demand?"

"I'm not going to get it. I'm not going to give them a chance to send it. I'm going to send them my own demand first."

"Which will be——?"

"That they deliver all the silver before they take away a single chest of opium."

"Do you think they'd agree to that?"

"We can try, can't we?"

"And what about the—the squeeze?"

"I never gave him a promise. The storm broke it up. So now I'll send to this mandarin and say that his suggestion is unacceptable and he'll have to be satisfied with some other gift."

"What?"

"I meant to bring that up. The ginseng."

Anne cleared her voice, quietly. He was not looking at her.

"Yes, I still have most of it," she said. "You may take it. But do you think this mandarin will accept such a gift in place of—of the one he originally asked for?"

"I don't know. But once again: we can try."

"See here, it's occurred to me that if you do get the silver on board and unload that—that stuff you call mud—why, we'd be just as low in the water as we are now, wouldn't we?"

"Probably. Maybe lower. Depends on how the silver is done up. The mud itself isn't very heavy, but those chests are."

"Then how do you expect to get out of here?"

"Suppose you let me worry about that when the time comes."

"What if Mr. Palmer brings back a report that we can't go back through that pass, even now?"

"Well, what if he does."

"Then you won't be able to send that demand to the mandarin."

"Sure I will. In fact, that's all the *more* reason to bluff."

She regarded him with perplexity, then admiration. She grinned. "And I was accusing you of not thinking things out," she said softly.

"I'm thinking very hard right now," he said, and took her into his arms and kissed her.

Kok Soo, facing them ten feet away, dropped the cable he'd been splicing and gaped in astonishment.

Abner scowled at him. "Get on with that job."

Early in the afternoon, about the time that the longboat came back out of the pass, the mandarin's men completed their occupation of the beach. Anne estimated them at two hundred, a formidable force. They did not, however, as Abner had expected, make any sort of demonstration. Though armed with all manner of hand weapons—they had no artillery that he could see—they did not brandish these. They set off no firecrackers, built no barricades. They did not even pitch tents.

"What can they *want*?"

"We'll find out."

Still Abner could not see the mandarin's umbrella, nor could he any longer see the bright bald head of Shap'ngtzai. These troops had no outposts; they didn't, for example, occupy the spit of land that came nearest the bark, as any competently led military force would have done. But perhaps they were awaiting orders. There was a certain amount of movement between the camp and the village; but for the rest the soldiers were curiously still.

Undeniably there was a faintly comic touch about them. Their weapons were old-fashioned, their garb grotesque. But Abner did not smile. Individually these men might be ridiculous, at least in Western eyes, but collectively, and whipped to a frenzy as they would be before attack, they'd go anywhere, do anything. Cut off from the rest of the world, they did not believe that they would ever be called to account for their crimes. They wouldn't have cared anyway. At a word from their lord they would kill a mariner with no more compunction than they'd feel in crushing a louse between their fingernails. If a strip of steel slid into your heart, the fact that its hilt was out-of-date wouldn't make you feel any better. If your throat was cut by a fantastically caparisoned trooper, it would be just as fatal as if the deed had been done by somebody more conventionally dressed.

They had a hot meal that noon, and all hands were on duty, but even then Abner did not relax his guard. He had sentries posted at five different places and he con-

H

tinually checked them. They had orders to report any unusual movement in the Chinese camp. Yet, as Ab told Anne, it was not a daytime attack he feared so much as a stroke in the night, when the soldiers might conceivably overrun the vessel, striking down everything right and left.

"But that would be plain piracy!"

"Well, there's plenty of that in these parts."

The moment he saw Pooch's face Abner knew that the pass was too shallow. Pooch shook his head, and handed his skipper a paper of figures which Ab scarcely glanced at.

"Not by a foot and a half in lots of places. Almost two feet in some."

Abner glanced towards the shore, still snatching what comfort he could get from the circumstance that there was no sort of boat in sight. He noted, too, that there seemed to be fewer soldiers now. Maybe this was only an observation party after all.

"Turn in, mister. You need the sleep."

"What about yourself?"

"I'm going to do the same. It'll be dark soon. Kok Soo'll command the deck. But not all night! I want you at sun-up."

"What are you going to do at sun-up?"

"Go ashore."

"No!" Anne's voice was sharp and her eyes flashed.

Abner had been skipper for little more than a week, but already he found himself bridling at a word of dissent. He glared at the girl.

"You may be the captain," she said, "but I've got some right as passenger, too. You can't just go away and leave me in a position like this."

"Ma'am, when I need your advice I'll——"

She had wheeled upon Pooch.

"You know what he means to do? He's going to tell them that they must pay over every tael of silver before they get any opium at all and that they've got to be satisfied with Nepalese ginseng for a squeeze. How d'you suppose they'll respond to *that*?"

"What was the original squeeze to've been?" Pooch asked.

"None of your business," said Abner.

"Why can't *you* do that, as his representative?" the girl persisted, still addressing Pooch. "Why does it have to be the captain? Why don't you go ashore instead?"

"Maybe I'd better," Pooch said slowly.

"Maybe the first thing you'd better do is learn where you stand on this ship, mister." Ab's voice was icy. He turned on his heel and walked forward, too angry to stand still.

Chapter Sixteen

IT WOULD be a dark night. The sunset was spectacular, with its streaked bright yellows, its strident orange; but it was brief. It held no note of softness, induced no languor. It did not soothe, as some sunsets do, nor did it exalt the imagination. Rather it had a murky quality. There was evil in it. The orb itself, a virulent red, showed exceedingly small, and it was slammed down into the sea as though by some terrible outer force, as a blacksmith plunges a red-hot horseshoe into water; you could almost hear the hiss. After that, clouds rippled across the sky, like a cloak expertly thrown. There was no touch of moonlight around the horizon, and scant room for any stars.

The soldiers on shore had pitched no tents, neither were they lighting any fires. More of them seemed to be leaving. They still showed no boat.

Abner sagged with weariness and all his muscles ached. He knew that he had been needlessly snappish, but he was too tired to care. When he returned to the after deck he passed Anne and Pooch without a word and went below. He fell into his bunk, clothes and all, even seaboots.

There was a step in the passage, Pooch Palmer's. The door was opened. But the mate did not enter. He stood there a moment, as if trying to make up his mind what to say; but Abner, eyes closed, didn't stir; and after a while Pooch went away, closing the door gently. That was the last thing Abner remembered.

Like so many sailors, he was accustomed only to short sleeps, naps. He was also accustomed to waking up fresh, with all his wits about him. He didn't drowse; he did not trail sleep behind him like ribbons of cigar smoke, but was instantly alert. This morning, however, it was different. He lay for a long time, as he supposed, groggy, like a man who had been drugged, before he fully realized that the skylight was dark. The glass was opaque, and had this been dawn, or had the moon been up, it would have shone a faint grey. Struggling to recover his senses, Ab was uneasy, haunted by hideous doubts. He found and opened his watch but it was too dark in the cabin to read it. He reached out—he lay in the lower bunk—and opened the cabin door.

In the light of the lamp in the passageway Ab looked again at his watch. Half-past two. Five bells.

He'd had every right to a long sleep, and had announced his intention of taking it. Nevertheless he was nervous, as full consciousness came, and he rose in haste.

Pooch Palmer's bunk was empty. There was nothing unusual in this. They were seldom both in the cabin at the same time.

He went out in to the passageway, ducking under the lamp. He knocked on the door of Anne Mackenzie's cabin, then opened it. She was not there. But Shen Ti was.

The little Chinese girl lay on her back in the lower bunk, motionless. Her eyes might or might not have been open —there was never any expression there anyway—but undoubtedly she knew that Abner was looking at her. Dreamily, languidly, with one tiny, exquisite yellow hand she drew open the top of her wrapper, exposing breasts enticingly firm. She pointed with a long-nailed forefinger first at one nipple, then at the other. Her lips were saying something over and over—with no sound.

Abner drew a deep breath. He stepped back.

Shen Ti sat up. Naked to the hips, she was pleading with him to stay. She extended round bare arms.

Abner closed the door.

When he reached the deck he saw that the moon was struggling to free itself from a cluster of soupy thick clouds low on the horizon. A breeze had sprung up, enough to scatter the surface of the water with cat's-paws, to sigh in the standing rigging, and, higher, to disperse the obstructing clouds. Soon it would be light.

He glanced over the side. The longboat was in the water, paintered to the bottom of the ladder, as it should have been, but Abner noted that the oars, docked, were wet.

Anne Mackenzie stood at the taffrail, staring towards the shore. It was nothing but a blur over there, a vague thickening of the darkness. No detail could be made out.

He went to her. She must have heard him but she didn't move.

" Where's Pooch? "

She kept staring at the beach she couldn't see.

" He went ashore," she answered at last.

" To see the mandarin? "

" To see the mandarin and tell him your terms."

" The fool ! " He grabbed her, spun her around. " You sent him ! To save me ! "

She was looking up at him now, her eyes luminous in the light of the binnacle lamp, her lips a little parted. She shook her head slowly.

" No, Abner, I didn't. It was his own idea. But I didn't do anything to stop him. Why should I ? "

" You might have waked me up ! "

" I might have," she agreed, " but I didn't."

It was as simple as that. He turned away, dropping his hands. He could not even feel anger. No, there was no reason why Anne should have tried to dissuade the boy. As for Pooch himself, his purpose was clear. If there was danger, he would face it first. It was like him. He was still trying to repay his hero, the older boy who years ago had rescued him from the Buckies. Pooch wouldn't have been dramatic about it. He did not have much sense. When he saw trouble coming he would simply lower his head and charge. Probably it had not even occurred to him that he might be sacrificing his own life.

"I'm sorry, Abner."

"Yes," he said.

"It—it'll be light soon."

"Yes. Did Kok Soo go with him?"

She nodded.

"As interpreter?"

"Of course."

"Who brought the longboat back?"

"The tindals."

He began to pace the deck, glancing from time to time at the cloud-smogged moon.

He tried to tell himself that maybe it would all be for the best. Pooch might win his point without serious trouble. If he was no diplomat, no bargainer to put up against a wily Oriental, conceivably his very innocence, his lack of guile might disarm the Lord of Namoo. Conceivably.

Ab tried to tell himself too that Kok Soo would somehow save the situation. He had considerable faith in Kok Soo, who saw a great deal without seeming to, and who assuredly knew his skipper's feeling for the mate. Ab would have sent Kok Soo in the first place as his sole representative had he not known that a Chinese would be unacceptable.

Ab was glad at least to see that they had not taken any weapons, not even their knives, which he now started to sharpen. A sailing man, officer or hand, hardly seemed a sailing man at all without his sheath knife, but the inhabitants of the Paracels might not know this. The sight of any sort of weapon, however small, however customary, might cause them to attack immediately, without ever having heard Pooch's message. It must have been Kok

Soo's idea to leave the knives behind. Pooch would never have thought of it.

Ab finished the job, then put his own knife, already razor-sharp, on the stone. After that he drew the charges from the three rifles and four pistols, and carefully reloaded these.

Anne, motionless by the taffrail, watched him. Suddenly she said in a low voice, " Here comes the moon, Abner."

He sprang to his feet, seizing the glass.

When the sun had set, with tropical abruptness, it had been like a whuffed-out lamp. When the moon rose upon that same scene it was like a lamp being lighted—though this time a lamp with a dirty globe. It did not seem so much that light came as that darkness went away.

Eagerly Abner Smith scanned the beach.

It was empty, bare. There were the rocks, the sedgy pools, the water that lapped a shelly edge, and scattered clumps of grass; but there were no men, and not even any signs of men. No, here was something. In the middle of the beach——

Abner almost dropped the glass. He tried to swallow and couldn't. His throat was tight. Sweat sprang out on his temples and under his eyes.

In the centre of that wild and desolate strand three poles, each about ten feet long, had been tied at the top and their bases spread, forming a tripod. It was like the support for an outdoor cooking pot, only larger. But it was not a pot that hung there. It was a man—or what had lately been a man. He hung upside down, tied by the ankles. The body swayed in the rising wind. It must have been warm, for blood still dribbled out of the place where once the head had been. The head itself, grinning up at the moon, was on the ground fifteen feet away.

There could not be any doubt as to the identity of this corpse. The great shoulders and ham-like hands, the blue coat, the striped jersey, the peaked cap on the beach, the horribly laughing head—all were those of Ralph Palmer, third mate, of Stonington, Connecticut.

The mandarin had made his answer.

Chapter Seventeen

FASCINATED, ABNER continued to stare at the gruesome scene. After a long time he looked away, his head down. Gradually he relaxed his grip. Slowly he turned.

He advanced towards her. "I'm going ashore," he said.

"Yes," she said. "I think you should."

The compliance, so prompt, touched him. Why had he ever squabbled with this girl? In every real emergency they thought alike. Their bickerings at the beginning of the voyage had been childish.

He said nothing of this, nor did he let it show in his face, but only nodded glumly.

"You'll be in charge while I'm gone," he said to the nearest of the two tindals. "Taken care of missy, chop-chop. Savvy?" He pointed to the longboat, still overside. "Catchem-up two-fella row-row. Savvy?"

He always felt silly talking pidgin, and never was sure

how much of it those two tindals understood. This one, at any rate, inclined a grave head, and Abner could only hope for the best.

To Anne Mackenzie Abner said, "Come below with me. I've got something to give you."

He showed her the two loaded pistols he was leaving—he holstered the other two in a bandoleer slung around his neck—and showed her how to reload these. He measured powder for her, and cut a supply of balls. He did the same with the three Kentucky rifles.

"Better keep these things in here," he said. He had them laid out on his own bunk, and he gave her a key to the cabin. "Your angel-from-heaven over there"—and he nodded towards the cabin across the passage—"might get to playing with them."

"Yes," she said, as she accepted the key. Then, more tartly, she added, "There is no need to be sarcastic."

"Sorry."

But this was not a quarrel. Though the subject of Shen Ti was still a sore one, each had come to realize that he'd been unfair to the other. In such circumstances, Abner refrained from commenting on the "princess's" habit of taking her clothes off at the drop of a hat. Anne, for her part, had come to know what Abner had said from the start—that Shen Ti was no seduced virgin, no fallen unfortunate victim of greedy opium merchants but a whore at heart as well as by profession. Anne would not admit her mistake aloud. She would not give the little creature up—and indeed, where else could Shen Ti have been lodged?—but she had come tacitly to agree on the need for watching her.

Now she nodded, and when they went out into the

passageway she locked the cabin door and put the key into the breast of her dress.

The rest of the *Forest's* small armoury consisted of three cutlasses. Abner took all of these, one in a scabbard at his side, the other two, naked, tucked under his left arm.

"There's no such thing as a shovel aboard," he explained, when Anne looked questioningly at him. "The burial will take time."

"I see."

The breeze that had sprung up was freshening to a wind, and the *Forest of Arden* rocked a little as he kissed Anne. They held one another, hard. But only for a moment.

Abner went up the ladder first. On deck they were reserved, business-like. Anne had only one suggestion—and she was careful to phrase it *as* a suggestion. She pointed to a stony spit of land that thrust itself into the lagoon nearest the bark, the spit the swivel gun was trained upon. It was very low, and held no vegetation at all and no high rock. Its farther end was a good two miles from the beach where Pooch Palmer's body hung.

"If you landed there it'd be a longish walk, but it would give you a chance to look things over—and they wouldn't be able to rush the boat."

"I see what you mean." Ab was trying to study the terrain behind the beach and at the same time refrain from looking at what remained of his mate. "It may be a trap."

Even with the tide out, the beach was not a deep one, though it was long. It was backed by a mass of those spiky high rocks that were the most notable characteristic of these islands, though none of them was to be seen on the spit, which could have been no more than a stone-studded sand-bar. These rocks were a dullish brown or dullish grey. They might have been and probably were coral. It was impossible to tell from the deck of the *Forest.* They were tall, thin, forbidding, and they jutted every-which-way. It was Abner's guess that some time not so long ago a tidal wave had engulfed these islands, or else a hurricane of unprecedented force had hurled seas clear across them, ripping them open, spewing chunks of what had been their floor in mad abandon this way and that, so that when it receded—perhaps as it did so scooping out this very lagoon in which the bark from Stonington floated—the rocks were left helter-skeltered like jackstraws.

Whatever the explanation, those boulders, rising like monstrous tombstones behind the beach, would afford the mandarin's men an incomparable hiding place. You could conceal a whole company behind them.

The mandarin's army had come, and unaccountably the mandarin's army had gone—all within a few hours. But had those soldiers, after having slain and mutilated the emissary from the skipper of the *Forest,* in truth withdrawn from that vicinity? Was it not possible that they had left a picked force, no more than ten or twelve, who would wait for the morning in the hope that the white devils would venture ashore to claim the carcass of one of their own? Was this, as Anne intimated, a trap?

He believed that it might be, that she could be right. She had horse sense, that slight, small woman. He was beginning to understand why Sir Gordon Mackenzie, a man noted on three continents for his hardheadedness, had picked her to study for him a commercial situation on the other side of the world.

"Aye," Abner said at last, "I'll go the round-about way."

An hour later he was exceedingly glad that he had made this decision.

The trouble with landing on the beach had been the possibility that he'd be rushed from behind those rocks the instant the boat grounded. He could not trust the Lascars. Ten to one they would row away in panic, leaving him to be slaughtered. Even if they resisted, what would they fight with?

So it was at the end of the rocky spit that he landed. He sent the boat back, having announced that he would signal for it when it was needed. It was as he walked down the spit, eyeing the beach where the body hung, that he decided not to approach that beach directly. If he did so he could fall into the same trap. Even if he saw them coming and ran out on the spit again, it was unlikely that he could outrun them all. A slip of the foot on this unfamiliar ground would be fatal. Besides, the boat could hardly get back to the point in time to take him off, even supposing that the Lascars were willing to get in so close.

No, his approach would be a circuitous one. He would go in among those gaunt rocks to see what he could see, and hear what he could hear, before he ventured out on the open beach.

The rocks, throwing so many shadows, appeared to offer refuge; yet Abner found that to go among them was like diving into a pool when you had no way of knowing how deep it was—or wasn't. Even to contemplate it made his muscles tight.

He glanced skyward and saw the moon. He glanced to

his right and was comforted by the sight of the *Forest of Arden* floating serenely in the middle of the lagoon.

He studied the gloom-wrapped area of rock before him. It gave no sign, and no sound came from out of it. He took a deep breath, and went in.

The transition from moonlight to deep shadow was like stepping into an unlighted house. It was as abrupt as though a door had been slammed shut behind him.

What's more, he sensed immediately that he was not alone. Somebody else was in there with him.

Chapter Eighteen

IN SUCH a place a knife was called for. A cutlass among these monoliths would be all but unswingable. Ab's pistols were Harrisons, heavy things with octagonal brass barrels and fishtail butts made of mahogany. Empty, each would make a good cudgel; but like all pistols they were touchy, and if held by the barrel when loaded might go off in your hand. Moreover, they were very noisy, and this occasion called for quietude.

No, the knife was the thing. He slipped it out of its sheath. The two loose sabres he laid on the ground, and after that he unbuckled the third one, lowering it as though on eggshells. He lifted off the bandoleer with the pistols.

He did not otherwise move, and scarcely breathed.

The moon was a feeble ally to-night. Since it had first thrown its light over the scene of horror on the beach, the sky had hazed considerably. Here among the upthrust stones the moon's murky glow made the shadows seem even more sable. And Abner prudently stuck to the shadows.

He was sure that he had heard something. He was waiting to hear it again. Soon he did.

It was the click of stone against stone, a sound that would have been inaudible on any but the stillest of nights. It might have been caused by a man walking very quietly, very carefully. It came from ahead of Abner, and a little to the left. Crouching, his knife held point forward like a sword, he started in that direction.

The footing was a danger. Pebbles could rattle together in such a way that, in this bouldered wilderness, they sounded like a blare of trumpets, or the firing of signal guns. Abner lowered his feet with the greatest care; but he wore seaboots, and soon he too, despite his caution, dislodged a stone.

He froze.

A breeze sighed among the rocks, while a short distance away, at the edge of the lagoon, the sea seemed to caress the sand, sibilantly reassuring it. Once he heard or thought he heard a slim *scree-ee* as though of a dry, strained rope. That could have been Pooch Palmer's halter, he reflected. He must be close to it, though he could not see even the lagoon itself from inside this stony forest. The only other sound was the far mumble of surf, so faint that it seemed to blend with the sighing of the wind.

Was there more than one man among these boulders?

Was there perhaps a whole party? He shook off this notion. If a trap had indeed been set, if many were here rather than only one, they would have seen him coming while he still was bathed in moonlight. Why should they have waited, then, for him to creep into the protection of the shadows? Why had they not shot him down in cold blood as he approached?

He answered that question himself: It might be that they wanted to take him alive in order to question him, in order to get certain information out of him. The Chinese were notorious for their tortures, and in such an out-of-the-way place a man like the mandarin of Namoo would be restrained by no legal or ethical bond, certainly not by the niceties of diplomatic etiquette.

It was a cramping thought, restrictive like a straight-jacket being tightened across his chest, under his arms; but still he sloughed it off. There was only one person here besides himself, he was sure. And that one person he would get. Abner knew a few questions of his own that he would like to hear answered. After what he had seen on the beach he was in no mood for loving kindness or turn-the-other-cheek. He took a fresh grip on his knife and found that his hand was sweaty. He waited. . . .

After a while he heard another sound. Surely it would have been hard to miss this one, a distinct click, again as of stone against stone, much louder than the previous ones. He thought he heard too a sharp intake of breath, as though in exasperation.

This came from straight ahead, maybe fifteen or twenty feet away. It was hard to gauge distance in that broken-up place.

Abner started towards it. As before, he kept to the shadows, slipping along the side of first this boulder, then that, never permitting so much as a toe to show itself in the light of the moon. He went slowly. His course was not direct—it couldn't be, in the circumstances—but he kept his general sense of direction, and soon he came to the spot from which, he would have sworn, the sounds had emanated.

There was nothing.

He did not know what he had expected. Conceivably he was overstrained, his nerves too taut. He stood motionless, upright by the side of a rock that reared fully twelve feet high.

He had been tensed against attack from any direction. He could have whirled this way or that, dodged, sidestepped, leaning either way, lashing out with his sheath knife. The one thing he had not anticipated was assault from *above*.

Whether his reason warned him or whether it was some atavistic instinct he was never to know. All he knew was that suddenly he was aware that somebody was dropping off the rock.

He threw himself sideways, twisting his head in time to catch a glimpse of the swooping shadow, the gleam of a knife.

He was struck in the left leg while falling, and he hit the earth with a thud; yet he managed to roll away and he got to one knee as a man came at him.

Abner rose, turning somewhat, reaching out with his left hand. He trusted to his senses rather than his sight. He could barely see the other man.

His hand caught a wrist, and he pushed it out and away, trying to twist it; but at the same time his own right wrist was seized.

They came together, chest against chest, with a violence that all but drove the breath out of them.

I

There was nothing unusual in the way they moved, for each in fact had played a classic knife-fighter's trick. The extraordinary thing was that they'd done it precisely together—and in the dark. Two ballet dancers, after rehearsing a *pas de deux* for many weeks, could not have bettered that timing.

The other man hooked a leg behind Abner's knees, pushing, so that when they fell he fell on top. Abner kept his legs together, for the other man was trying to kick him in the groin. Ab's left arm was pinioned between the two of them, and for the moment he had no use of it, but he butted up vigorously with his head, catching the man on the point of the chin. There was some relaxation of the grip on his right wrist. He heaved violently, at the same time jolting upwards with his left shoulder. Now he was on top, or almost on top. He kept lifting that left shoulder, catching the chin again and again. Moreover, there was rock back of the other's head now—the same rock from the top of which, after tossing a stone to lure Abner on, he had leaped.

Two—three—four—then one more time.

It was inglorious, but effective. The grip on his wrist weakened perceptibly, all but fell away. Fearful of a ruse, Abner did not relax his own grip, but he did get to one knee, yanking his knife hand away. He fumbled for and found the other's throat, and he pressed this with the point of the knife.

"*Don't move!*"

It was a stupid thing to say to a Chinese, but he hoped that the other, if conscious, would understand the tone of voice.

Abner could make out only a blur, but he did see the

eyes opened; and the voice, a good Yankee voice, hit his ears like music.

"Who the hell are *you*?"

Abner almost smiled. "Could it be, could it just be," he said, "that the last time I heard that voice was through a speaking trumpet?"

"It could if you're off the *Forest of Arden.* I'm Austin third mate of the brig *Firefly*, out of Boston. Say, that was a skunk's trick, blowing away your rigging."

"It was."

"You understand, I was only obeying orders. Captain MacHarg stayed out of sight, but he was only a few feet away all the time."

"Well, what's done's done. Where is *Firefly* right now, mister?"

"At the bottom of the South China Sea. Say, take that thing away from my throat. So you're off the *Forest*, eh?"

"Aye."

"She afloat?"

"Aye."

"Then I want to meet your skipper."

"You have."

"Oh . . . Well, take me aboard, captain."

Abner rose. He sheathed his knife. Spread-legged, thumbs hooked into his belt, he looked around. Through a rift in the rock he could see his vessel, his world, as graceful as a bird that had alighted there a moment before and might fly away again a moment hence.

"I'll take you aboard," he promised. He started towards the spot where he had left his other weapons. "But we have something to do first."

Austin rose. A big man, sweaty and heavy, he was confused.

"Something important, captain?"

"Something mighty important. Come on."

Chapter Nineteen

THE JOB immediately at hand—cutting down the body, searching it, composing the limbs, trying to replace the head in some sort of decent position—Abner took for himself. The knuckles of both hands were skinned, suggesting that Pooch had punched a few faces before being pinned to earth. There was a great deal of blood, all now either dry or fast drying. The pockets yielded nothing. Abner had half expected to find some manner of insulting message, but the mandarin's men must have assumed that the body itself, exposed as it was, constituted the strongest possible insult.

This work Abner did in a controlled fury, rapidly, silently, his head averted. The digging of the grave was different. Here Austin could help.

Brought out into the open, Austin proved to be a tall, rawboned young man, bigger even than Ab Smith. His feet were bare, and they were cut and bleeding. He was so weary that he could hardly stand. His clothes, besides being wet, were badly slashed. His hair and his whiskers were matted with dirt. His eyes were bloodshot. He was still dizzy from the battering Abner had given him. When he was handed a cutlass and told to dig he said, "Do we have to do this now?"

"We do. Get busy. And tell me about it while you dig."

It was like two prisoners of war: though neither had any actual authority, the one of higher rank told the other what to do. The island was, in a very real sense, an enemy prison. And Austin, the mate, hesitated for no more than a moment. Talking seemed to do him good.

The *Firefly*, Abner learned, had been making a course perilously close to the Paracels when caught by the storm. It had piled up on a reef about half a mile off the far end of this island. Most of the crew went down with it, only one boat-load making the shore. Austin had been in command of this boat, six men besides himself.

"Americans?"

"Well, U.S. citizens anyway."

Abner nodded. It was the same sort of crew *Forest* had originally carried, the crew that had deserted in Calcutta. Yankee ships generally were officered by Yankees but manned by men from all parts of Europe, men who, attracted by superior wages, contrived to carry some manner of U.S. birth certificates, all forged.

"Go ahead," said Ab.

"Well, the sons of bitches gave us a lovely welcome, I'll say that for them. Could hardly wait for us to stagger ashore before they had their hands in our pockets. Then they stripped the shoes off us."

"To keep you from running away?"

"That could have been the reason, but personally I think it was just because they wanted the shoes."

"Go on."

"It was only by the grace of God we made it. But *they* had some stout boats, and I begged them to lend me one so's we could go back and try to take some of the others off. She was pounding to pieces out there. But they wouldn't let me have a boat. They got out there fast enough themselves, though, hoping to grab some of that Malwa."

"And she's a complete wreck, you think?"

"Captain, there ain't so much as a hatful of splinters left. The bastards," he said feelingly. "They didn't even give us anything to eat until they got back, and when they did, what was it? God only knows. It tasted like seagulls' guts. Maybe it was."

"Get on with your story," Ab said, "and keep your voice down."

Not until near noon had anybody taken the trouble to notice them again, and by that time they were more dead than alive. Abner gathered that this neglect had been due to several things: the callousness of a wild island people; the customary Chinese contempt for "white devils," especially when they were in distress; vexation at their failure to profit by a shipwreck, and a rich one; and last but not least, dissension among their leaders.

"There was this little fella with the button on his cap," said Austin, "and there was also a baldy-head with shoulders this wide."

"Shap'ngtzai?"

"That could be it. Something like that. Anyway, they sure didn't like each other, those two. I couldn't get a word in edgeways. Not that they'd have understood it even if I did. But they might at least have offered us something to eat and a place to lie down."

"What were they quarrelling about?"

"You."

"Oh?"

"Seems you piled up or almost did just about the same time as us. Or anyway *some* vessel did, and it wasn't hard to guess that it was *Forest of Arden*. As best I could get it, the old man had ordered a whole army to march against you, and Baldy had countermanded that order, so nobody knew where they stood. Baldy was warning the old geezer that you might be a tough nut to crack, and anyway he was saying you'd made some kind of deal with them and why didn't they stick to that?"

"Wait a minute," Abner interrupted. "How did you know all this?"

"One of my men, the second cook, is part Chinese, and he understands some of the lingo. He could give us the general drift of it anyway."

"I see."

"Well, they finally got around to giving us this stuff that tasted like something scraped off the floor of a bird-cage. But it was manna from heaven as far as we were concerned. We finished off every bit of it. Then they locked us up in a kind of wooden cage. It wasn't much. Nothing but a bare floor, and wooden bars. I figured that if I could only keep the boys awake we could dig our way out as soon as it got dark. It didn't look as if they'd post very smart guards. They were a sloppy lot in the first place, and they had us here on an island——"

"That's deep enough," Abner said, nodding to the grave. "Now take him by the legs. I'll get him under the arms."

"So I just high-tailed it out of there."

"Simply ran away?"

"That's about it. I picked a time when there was some big fuss about something, just when they were forcing the boys into that cage. I don't think anybody even noticed me, though they may well have missed me since. The reason I knew which direction to take was because I'd seen them waving this way so many times with their arms while they were arguing."

"And you came the whole distance on bare feet?"

"Well, I admit I didn't travel very fast. Fact is, I could hardly move at all. And several times when people came along I had to hide for a while. And when finally I got among those rocks over there I was lost for fair. Then you came along, and I didn't know whether you was friend or enemy, but naturally I bet on enemy."

"Naturally."

"And I could tell from the way you moved that *you* was stalking *me.*"

"I was sure trying to."

"So I climbed up on a rock and dropped a pebble to fetch you, and when you came along I fell on top of you. Only you moved too fast."

"All right, that's enough now," Abner said, and rose. "Shut up. I want to pray."

"Now look, captain, we ain't got the time to——"

"*I said shut up, didn't I?*"

Austin backed away. "All right, captain. Sure. Sure."

Abner knelt by the side of the crude grave and prayed, as had always been his habit, aloud; but he kept his voice very low.

When he rose, after smoothing the dirt and stones again

—he would not mark the grave for fear that it would be desecrated—he turned again to Austin.

"Come along, mister. This is going to be hard on your feet, but I can't help that. We've got work to do."

"Aren't we going aboard of your ship, captain?"

"No. We're going back to that cage."

Chapter Twenty

THOUGH THERE was no sign of the sun itself, daylight already was drizzling down among the boulders like moon rays through the lattice in a garden. The stars had been washed off the sky. The air was chill.

Abner paused on a slight rise of ground after they had emerged from the rocky wilderness, and looked back. The lagoon, which had been glass, now was chipped with wavelets. *Forest of Arden* showed as no more than a blur, a thickening of the darkness, though her forepeak and mainpeak were touched by the opalescence of dawn. He shook his head. He hated to leave Anne there and go even farther from her, but he had a job to do for a dead friend.

The going was hard. For the most part the ground was level, or nearly so, but it was strewn with dark, sharp stones. Austin, his socks already worn away, his bare feet bruised and badly cut, could scarcely walk at all. It became apparent now why the villagers had removed the shoes from their captives. After less than a mile Abner stopped, removed his sea-boots, and handed them to his companion. Abner did not do this out of Christian charity; he did it because he needed the services of Austin, and he couldn't count on the man in his present condition. Austin understood the spirit of the giving. Without so much as a nod of gratitude, though he winced when he did so, he pulled the boots over his bleeding bare feet. And the two men resumed their walk.

Now it was agony for Abner, whose socks very soon were cut to shreds. There was no avoiding the stones. Near the shore the ground consisted of nothing else; but even farther inland, when in the growing daylight the travellers came upon small scrubby fields and vegetable patches, the stones, though fewer and more widely scattered, were as pesky as ever, appearing where least expected.

Even the houses in this land of shards and boulders— at least such peasant huts as Austin and Abner came upon —were made of stone. These were low and dingy, and appeared to shrink into the hard earth, suggesting Eskimo dwellings rather than homes on a semi-tropical island. So drab were they, and so small and low, that it was difficult not to stumble upon them. With the spread of sunrise, columns of smoke were appearing against the sky, and these served as warnings. Even so, the two men did not go entirely unseen. Once they were hailed from within a hut, and they hurried on, not looking back, pretending that they had not heard. Dogs barked at them twice.

Fortunately the one farmer who later chased them did not have a dog. A large, shaggy, uncouth fellow in blue, wearing an enormous pyramid hat made of rattan, he saw them first; he shouted at them, and immediately charged, with a pitchfork held in both hands. The pitchfork was a formidable weapon; Ab had nothing better than his cutlass to fend it off with, Austin nothing better than a knife. And they doubted that the farmer would dare attack them single-handed unless he was sure that he'd soon be joined by others. They ran as fast as they could, stumbling out of a field of low, fat haycocks, then dodging back into it and circling several of the cocks so as to get out of sight of the farmer, whom they heard panting behind them. Finally they dived right into one of the stacks.

The dry chaff sifted into the chinks of their clothing, tickling them; and it was difficult not to sneeze when a sneeze might have meant their lives.

The farmer was tenacious. He lingered in the field of haycocks for at least twenty minutes, and they could hear him stamp from place to place, hear him talk to himself in a low, angry voice, hear him plunge the pitchfork periodically into the haycocks around them.

Even when he had departed they gave him a good ten minutes, while their eyes watered, their noses ran, and their skins itched almost beyond endurance. At last they crawled out, and saw the farmer in the next field, tedding grass. He still shook an angry head as he muttered to himself. They gave him a wide berth.

This episode meant a serious loss of time. Yet it was unlikely that even without it they would have reached the village before the coming of day, as Abner, not knowing about those stones, had hoped. When it got so light as to be dangerous they found themselves in a peculiarly vulnerable, exposed spot. They were trudging a narrow country track or lane that could hardly be called a road. It was lined on one side by a stone wall. There were no trees or bushes nearby, and.no barns.

They stopped, to look around, and heard a shout from a little behind them, on the left. Abner whipped out his cutlass, but when he turned he knew it was no use. There were six of them, one an officer, and they had muskets. They were a few feet back, on the other side of the wall. At that distance, even an islander pointing an antiquated firearm could scarcely miss. And six of them certainly couldn't. The officer motioned for Abner to drop his blade, and Ab, sighing, did so.

Half an hour later they were thrust into a cage with high wooden bars and no floor, which they shared with seven men who were sound asleep.

Abner's sea-boots were taken from Austin. "Up to their old tricks, the bastards," grumbled the mate. "Well, here I am right back where I started from." Then he dropped to the ground and instantly fell asleep.

Abner was not long in following him. He was mistily aware, just at first, that somebody had entered the cage and was standing over him, probably staring down at him; but he couldn't care, and did not open his eyes. Presently the person went away.

When he awoke it was dusk, and the first thing he saw was Kok Soo. The bos'n had been beaten. His face looked like beef turning bad. One eye was closed. Blood that had flowed from a dozen untended places on his arms, neck, and hands had long since clotted and dried, but it was none the less ugly. Pain still lingered in his eyes, but he remembered his manners and bowed before his skipper.

" Tell me what happened," Ab said.

Because his English was limited, the bos'n kept the story short. He and Pooch had been reasonably well received and had been conducted to this village, where they were arraigned before the Lord of Namoo and Shap'ngtzai, the former being seated, as became his rank.

Kok did not try to colour his tale, adjectives being no specialty of his, but Ab gathered that the mandarin on this occasion had been a much more splendid sight than he was aboard the *Forest*. Shap'ngtzai, on the other hand, was about the same.

" Allee-samee   hate?"   Ab   asked.   " Baldy-Namoo hatem?"

" Hatem," Kok Soo soberly confirmed.

" Just what I said," put in Austin. " They were ready to cut one another's throats. Well, I wish they had. The bastards."

The pair from the bark, it could be deduced, had interrupted the very quarrel Austin had seen the beginning of. When they arrived in the village Shap'ngtzai and the mandarin still were snarling at one another over the way to treat the *Forest of Arden*. Pooch Palmer had delivered his message, through Kok, at the worst possible moment. The mandarin had flown into a rage, shrieking commands that Kok with his limited knowledge of the court language could not understand. Soldiers then had closed in on Pooch, who began to fight back. Shap'ngtzai had protested but was overruled. Kok Soo had tried to interfere, but soon he too was surrounded by soldiers. He never saw what happened to the mate. Weaponless himself, he couldn't fight. So, being sensible, he had thrown himself on the ground and covered his vital parts as best he could and taken his beating. He did not expand on this theme. Now he asked about Pooch.

"They cut his head off," Abner said.

Kok nodded. Though he had been fond of Pooch, as Ab knew, he was too polite to show grief. His only expression was one of mild astonishment, as though he wondered why they had not done the same thing to him.

What they had done was beat him until he ceased to twitch and then toss him into this cage, which, when the soldiers had departed, he found he shared with six men.

Kok must have missed Austin by no more than a matter of minutes. Not that it made any difference—now.

As far as Abner could make out, Austin had not been missed. Ab also was ignored by the jailers, who it would seem scarcely even noticed that there were nine men in the cage now instead of the original seven. Villagers surrounding the cage stared and sometimes giggled and sniggered at the discomfiture of the white devils, making a particular holiday of it when one of them was obliged to relieve himself; but the jailers themselves were apathetic. Yet the jailers, if not alert, still were *there*.

"They'll go to sleep after a while," Austin predicted.

"I hope so," muttered Ab.

These two had examined the bars Austin had lifted out to make his own escape. The mate from the *Firefly* had been careful to replace the bars, so as not to attract attention. It would be easy to open them again, once the prisoners had any privacy at all. The men were all awake now, an uninspired lot but able-bodied. They were not noisy, but they were extremely hungry and desperate to get back aboard a ship. Moreover, they were used to taking orders, as Austin and Abner were used to giving them.

"It's just a matter of waiting now," said Abner Smith. "Our time will come."

Chapter Twenty-One

SHAP'NGTZAI WOKE, belched thoughtfully, glowered at the ceiling. The captain of the guard, who was also captain of the port, had a hangover. Yet except in cases of alarm, this was his usual time to rise, wine or no wine, court tension or no tension. At first light—not, strictly speaking, dawn—he needed no awakener.

He swung his legs over the edge of the boards that served him as a bed, and sat up. He was as hard as those boards. At a glance one might have supposed him fat, for he was short and very broad, and his chest and shoulders were built like a gun turret. But no part of him quivered. He was a hard man—hard-muscled, hard-boned, and with eyes of adamant—and right now he was naked, for night garments were not the custom at Namoo of the Paracels in that year of Our Lord 1835. He gleamed like ivory, from his stubby strong toes to the top of his hairless head.

He belched again, then called for a servant. He heard somebody move in the anteroom, and assumed that the sound in the next room had been made by one of his attendants. Even before he relieved himself he wished to order breakfast and a horn of rice wine, hoping to temper his headache, to lessen that hammering at the back of his eyeballs.

He rose. The rings in his ears—the only things he wore —swung back and forth. He scratched his buttocks, one with each hand. He called a command.

The answer was muffled, and the voice was not familiar. Even then the captain of the guard suspected nothing. He did not glance through the slats of his sleeping chamber window, to be sure that sentries still paced the compound. He did not worry about assassination, not because he thought the Lord of Namoo above such methods, but because he did not believe that there was a man on the island with the courage to tackle him alone, even when he was asleep. And he was right.

The anteroom door was opened, and a white devil came in. He held a cutlass in one hand, a cocked pistol in the other; but he did not point the pistol at anything in particular, and the blade, though certainly bare, was not raised. He was followed by another white devil and by a Chinese, who was not, however, an islander. Each of these held a cutlass.

Shap'ngtzai's first fuzzy impression was that the mandarin, his enemy, had somehow contrived to bribe the whole company of white devils to do the deed none of his own followers dared to do. He snorted in disgust. He hunched his shoulders, planted his bare feet firmly on the floor, clenched his fists. He had nothing to fight with, but he meant to fight.

"Good morning, sir," said Abner Smith. "We'd like to have a talk with you."

Shap'ngtzai could not understand the words, but the

tone of voice was plain enough. Also, in the dim light, he had by now recognized the first of these white devils—the captain of the ship the mandarin had boarded. Shap'ngtzai trusted his own intuition. He did not believe that this captain would cut a man down in cold blood.

He put a palm to his forehead, rolling his eyes ceiling-wards. He jiggled a little on the balls of his feet. He pointed to the door of the private closet, then pointed to a certain part of his anatomy. Not for a moment of this time did he lose his dignity.

Abner grinned.

"Why, sure," he said. "Go ahead. We can wait a few minutes."

But time did count and on Shap'ngtzai's return the strain of talking through an interpreter had never before been so wearing. In a little while, a half-hour at most, the garrison would rise. The sentries would be changed. The sundry lieutenants would appear here to report to their captain. Somebody in passing might glance into the cage and notice that two of the prisoners were missing. The alarm would be sounded.

The three thus far had enjoyed good luck. They had not been seen nor had their escape been discovered. The soldiers of this island outpost—a bored, degenerate lot—still slept, no doubt dreaming of the butchery and loot when on the morrow the crew of the second western vessel would surrender—or else, in trying to escape, would go aground in the pass, to be ravaged at leisure. Unaccustomed to opposition, they had forgotten how to be alert. Moreover, their masters were squabbling, which was bad for morale. Gliding like shadows, Abner and Austin and Kok Soo had entered the village without challenge, had

K

approached the "fort" unseen, had all but stepped upon a couple of slumbering sentries in order to climb the main gate, had overcome and bound another sentry, less sleepy, inside the compound, and finally, and almost without a sound, had surprised and gagged the single attendant in the anteroom of the captain—all this in a very short time and without any hitch. This luck couldn't last. And now they chafed, when minutes were so precious, before the barrier that language raised.

"Tell him. . ." Then there would be the laborious business of getting the message into Kok Soo's head. The bos'n was not stupid; but aboard ship, where he usually knew what an order would be even before it was issued, he had fallen into the habit of guessing at a great deal of the English bellowed at him. Here he had to think. "Tell him . . ." Once he had comprehended the words, to his own satisfaction anyway, Kok Soo would sit motionless for a minute or two, mumbling to himself, doubtless rephrasing the message into a language that the captain of the guard could perhaps understand.

The return, of course, was the same process in reverse. "He say . . . He say . . ."

Moreover, Shap'ngtzai would not even consent to parley until he'd had his breakfast. They released the attendant long enough to permit him to bring a bowl of rice with a dark viscid fish sauce, and a horn of wine.

The horn—a Viking touch, grotesquely out of place in this tropical setting—was empty, and the rice bowl too, before Shap'ngtzai, ponderous but finicky, at last consented to nod his permission to speak. Thereafter the conversation was largely one-sided, Abner Smith talking earnestly, rapidly, and with many gestures, directly facing the captain of the guard, while Kok Soo did all he could to keep up and interpret. Shap'ngtzai contented himself with an occasional grunt of assent, and steadily, while picking his teeth with a gold toothpick, stared at Abner.

The plan that Abner proposed was an elaborate one, and the captain of the guard, though by no means timid, took a little time to digest it. At last he laid aside the toothpick. He rose, his earrings swinging. Still staring at Abner, approval loud in his eyes, he let forth a stream of incomprehensible words.

For some moments the interpreter was silent, pondering. Then he brightened. He looked at Abner. "He say 'yes'."

Abner too rose. "Good. Let's get started then."

Chapter Twenty-Two

THERE WERE skippers—known as "drivers", though they were called other things in the forecastle—who believed that the only good sailor was a busy one. Religious men for the most part, they were fond of quoting "Satan finds work for idle hands to do", unaware that this was not from the Bible. To them, the carving of scrimshaw or a simple snooze in the sun were sins. If the deck had just been holystoned, all sail only just set, and everything that could be polished polished, and still hands lounged, spinning yarns—why, damn it, holystone the deck again!

Drivers were not popular. Sometimes they were affable

enough ashore, but fiends in human form at sea. You seldom found one aboard a sealer or whaler, for those vessels, floating slaughterhouses, were notoriously slow and lubberly, stinking, greasy, dirty and what they had most of, the whalers especially, was time. The clippers, however, were crowded with them. "I don't spare myself," a driving captain would say defensively, neglecting to mention that he owned a lay in the vessel he commanded, or at least part of her cargo, "so why should I spare those lazy louts?" Customarily no hands were present when he so spoke.

Abner had often wondered whether he would fall into the class of drivers if and when he got a command. As mate he had been known as a bucko—a hard case, an officer who would stand for no nonsense—but that might only have been because, as a conscientious man, he was carrying out orders. His experience told him that a salt could change overnight when he was moved from the forecastle aft, as he could be transformed again when he got a command.

So far, Abner had been harsh; but that was no real test. His ascent to a skippership had been a fluke. He had faced out freakish weather. With only one officer to back him, and short-handed, he had commanded a crew that through no fault of his own was half-mutinous and wholly unreliable.

Abner liked to think that he would not be a driver, ordinarily. Certainly, however, he was one when he took charge of this land command. Time was the most important thing in the world, and Abner would tolerate no further delay. He was ruthless. He kicked, coaxed, and spoke in a voice that splashed with acid.

Abner could hardly feel his feet, made numb by weariness, and he had to bat his eyes hard, again and again, to keep them from sliding closed. The squat, sturdy Kok Soo was impassive, as always, but his step was not certain and he often stumbled. Austin in the worst condition of the three, might have been a somnambulist; his senses seemed nine-tenths submerged, and once, when he slipped to his knees, it took two men to raise him and push him gently on his way.

On the other hand, the six men they'd rescued from the cage were stupefied with sleep. Not too intelligent in the first place, they were confused, frightened. They were submissive when herded, but they could not be trusted out of sight. They reminded Abner of many a clump of poppy-drowsed pipers he had driven out of opium dens. They were, as Austin had said, a polyglot crowd. Nor did they seem keen about being rescued. Still, Ab hoped that when the time came they would fight. He hoped . . .

The mist that had crept in from the sea both hindered and helped. It made the individual members of the party hard to keep track of, increasing the need for bunching and for alertness against straggling; but at the same time it made them, from a short distance, resemble any of the villagers, so that though several times they passed within a few yards of early risers they were not recognized as white devils and no alarm was raised.

The mist would not last long. It hung motionless, except where it was disturbed. It didn't drift. The sky was being washed clear of stars as a blackboard is erased of chalk marks. It would be a clear, hot morning. The sun in the east, struggling to rise low over the sea, soon would burn this vapour away. But by that time the escaped prisoners would be far from the village—they hoped.

Progress was precarious. There were no trees, but there were rocks that reared, enormous, out of the mist. Once, a rickety bamboo-and-nipa-thatched hut seemed to swoop upon them, as though seeking to engulf them. Once they all fell down a deep gully, stirring up a clatter of stones; but either this was not heard or no attention was paid to it.

The countryside was all rocks, no roads, no hills or other landmarks. The surf sounded on almost every side, so that the direction of the nearest shore could not be definitely known. They might as well have been blind. They had no compass. Austin had entered this village twice and now was leaving it for the second time, but even he, his senses dulled by fatigue, was lost. Yet they did not dare to stop.

When the alarm at last sounded behind them, signifying the discovery of the jail-break, it came as a relief. They knew that pursuit would not be too prompt. Shap'ngtzai had agreed to that. They would be given time to reach the other side of the island. They might even get a chance to refresh themselves for the coming fight.

Abner had been blunt with the captain of the guard. "It's your life or the mandarin's," he had pointed out. The mandarin had Peking on his side, but Peking was a long way way off. The captain of the guard could set up an independent kingdom in the Paracels. He could be a monarch. The imperial government would never send a fleet against him; it wouldn't be worth their while. On the other hand, if he did not act soon, if he didn't grab this opportunity while it was being offered, he was going to wake up one morning and find himself not merely without a headache but without even a head.

The captain of the guard, when this had been translated, nodded, his earrings ajog. Abner was absolutely right.

The "escape" was easily engineered. Shap'ngtzai himself escorted the group to a small door in the wall of the compound, and unlocked this for them. He even considered giving them his personal attendant as a guide, but decided against this when it occurred to him that if by chance the little party should fall afoul of some soldiers the presence of such a person in their midst would look very bad for him, Shap'ngtzai.

"He say: that happen, he kill us all."

"Sure, Kok. Sure, I got that. Tell him to go on."

Shap'ngtzai did, however, get them five long, cumbersome, old-fashioned muskets, together with half a dozen powder horns, a bagful of percussion caps, and plenty of lead. They had, in addition, three cutlasses, two pistols, and four knives. A pitiful force, yes. But they did not plan to conduct this revolution unassisted.

The garrison at Namoo was divided between those who would fight for their captain and those who were the mandarin's men. However, there were not many fanatics on either side. The greater part of the garrison probably didn't give a damn.

The captain of the guard, called upon to organize a pursuit, would pick the most devoted of the mandarin's men, the die-hards. The less rabid royalists, who yet might bear watching, would be told to encircle the shores of the island and confiscate every small fishing boat, the ostensible purpose of this move being to prevent the fugitives from getting to another island where it would be troublesome to capture them, though of course its actual purpose was to get rid of these men when the final battle came.

Shap'ngtzai would then put together a follow-up force officered by his own adherents. The original pursuit squad, the mandarin's men, would have orders to attack the white devils on sight. The support force, under Shap'ngtzai in person, would be for mopping-up purposes.

Abner's plan called for one of the fleeing nine men to hurry ahead—he had picked Kok Soo for this assignment —and from the end of the rocky spit that stuck out into the lagoon signal for the longboat to be sent ashore from the *Forest of Arden*. Once aboard the bark, Kok Soo would take command of the stern-chaser, its swivel gun already loaded with grape and laid and aimed for the middle of the spit.

The other eight fugitives would go out to the end of the spit, where the pursuing mandarin's men would have them trapped. They would then simulate panic, seemingly having counted upon a boat that was not there. The mandarin's men, sensing an easy kill, would close in. And Kok Soo would open up with the swivel gun.

A whiff of grapeshot, as Napoleon once pointed out, can do wonders. The soldiers almost certainly would be taken by surprise, and Abner's men would rush them, driving them back among the tall rocks, where Shap'ngtzai's follow-up force would fall upon and annihilate them.

This was the plan. From the beginning, things went wrong with it.

The alarm goings behind them had caused them to alter their course, only to have it proved once again that sounds in such weather are deceptive. When the mist lifted sufficiently for them to see any appreciable distance, they learned that they were in fact far over towards the middle of the island. This meant a longer walk, and the walking was nasty. It also meant time. If the mandarin's men got to the *Forest of Arden*'s lagoon first, all would be lost. No alternative plan had been agreed upon. There had not been time. Even if Abner's tough tars got there first, still possible, they would have little or no chance to rest their feet, dash sea water upon their faces, look to their weapons, answer nature, and select firing positions among the rocks.

Nor was Kok Soo the man to outrush the others. He simply wasn't up to it. His spirit might be indomitable, but his legs weren't strong enough. It was all he could do to keep up, much less hasten ahead.

Austin was even more tired. The others, unacquainted with the layout of the lagoon, like Austin were unknown to those aboard the bark, so that their signal for a boat might be ignored.

In other words, it was now up to Abner himself to go.

He handed Austin one of his pistols, retaining the other for signalling purposes. He glanced around, like a man about to make a plunge into unknown water. And then, somehow, he broke into a trot. And somehow he kept it up.

He sweated, for it was getting warm as the sun rose, and the air was muggy. He stumbled again and again, several times falling asprawl, so that his knees and elbows and the heels of his hands became badly cut. But he kept on.

The *Forest of Arden*, anchored fore and aft, was a lovely, assured craft even in that light. There was more mist over the lagoon than over the land, though it was low. *Forest's* waterline could not be distinguished from the end of the spit, but the rest of her was plain enough, her hulk and rigging etched against a sky that was all pigeon-neck pastels.

But—he could see nobody move there. He could see no stir. There should have been a shout to greet his appearance on the spit, for he had left orders that the shore should be watched.

Troubled, he took out his pistol. He examined its priming, and cocked the striker. He was raising the weapon when something in the water not far away caught a corner of his eye. He turned.

Not fifty feet from where he stood, a freak of the mist opened a small space for a moment, revealing the longboat. It floated free. The oars were shipped, the thole pins in place. But there was nobody in the boat, which almost immediately was swathed in mist again and blotted from sight.

That eerie glimpse fastened like an icy hand around Abner's heart. He was sure that something had happened aboard ship.

Still no sign came from the ship itself. Nobody moved there. Once again he raised his pistol—when a shot rang out.

Mist or no mist, that shot undoubtedly came from the *Forest of Arden*, off the stern of which there now rolled a round yellowish blob of gunsmoke.

There was a scream—then there was silence.

Chapter Twenty-Three

A BNER STOOD transfixed. Except for that cloud of gunsmoke, which soon thinned and slowed and lost its identity by merging with the mist, there was no movement on the bark. Except for the pounding of surf far away and the high, thin squeak of gulls, there wasn't any sound.

He looked back. Nobody was in sight. He studied the ship again. Nothing stirred there.

He uncocked the pistol and placed it in a conspicuous place on a stone. It would never do to take that into the water. Hours would be needed, afterwards, to get it back into working condition. But those who followed him might find a use for it.

He took off his jacket. He gave a hitch to his belt and strode into the water, which was unexpectedly cold and made him catch his breath.

Abner more than once had marvelled that so few sailors could swim. He supposed that this might be accounted for by the fact that many of them, lured by fond dreams of the sea, came down to the shore from inland places. Those who really knew the sea often avoided it as much as they were able to, in Abner's experience. However, he had a hard time believing that anybody could not swim. He couldn't remember having learned, any more than he could remember having learned to walk or to talk. He had virtually crawled out of his cradle to fall into Long Island Sound, and always took swimming for granted. This does not mean that he enjoyed it. Swimming for pleasure, for the exercise, would have seemed silly to him, a small boy's diversion not fit for a man. Nevertheless, and even in this cold water, even with his clothes on and the scabbarded cutlass slapping his thigh and his knees as he kicked, he could have swum clear to the *Forest of Arden* if necessary.

It was not necessary. He had remembered the approximate location of the longboat, and he swam slowly, looking to right and left. He was quiet, not lifting his arms above the surface.

The whole world was hushed that morning. Swimming silently, completely out of touch with everything, surrounded by vapour, he was now too low to see either ship or shore. He had nothing whatever to go by, and he knew that, just as a man lost in the woods can unwittingly walk in circles, so a man can swim in circles too. Had he been long like that he might have felt the tug of panic, but he came upon the longboat in a matter of minutes.

He swam slowly around it, still careful not to splash. The boat was in good condition, at least from the outside, but seven or eight feet of its painter trailed from its bow. That painter was stout quarter-inch line. It was new. It had not been frayed or worn away—it had been cut.

He went amidships on the larboard side, still swimming quietly, got a good grip on the gunnel, and heaved himself up.

What he saw were two axes, a water cask, a biscuit tin, three opium pipes, four sheath knives, a long, serpentine-bladed kris, a powder horn, a bullet mould, a large chunk of lead—and Shen Ti.

There was blood on the kris.

The reason he had not seen the little Chinese girl from

the spit was that she was seated, cross-legged, between two of the thwarts, and her head was not as high as the gunnel. As always, she did not look real. She suggested some temple ornament, a doll made of porcelain and paint, a lacquered idol. She turned her head, close to his. He did not think that her eyes were open, but she gave him a long, slow, sleepy smile, a smile that lingered for a long time after the lips had ceased to hold it.

"You take—Shen Ti," she sing-songed, very low. "Me Shen Ti—you take."

She must have been conscious of the unreality of her appearance, and, eager to prove that she was in fact a woman, all woman, she pressed her hands under her breasts, lifting them, causing them to look larger than they were. At the same time she started to hitch up her dress, exposing bare legs.

Abner Smith wriggled aboard. "You keep your clothes on," he barked. "We got no time for that now."

He looked around, and nodded. "Somebody was planning to jump ship, eh? Maybe three or four of the boys. Maybe all of them."

The pipes, the way the food was stored, the fact that it was food obtainable from the forward quarters and therefore accessible to members of the crew made it clear to Ab that somebody had planned to desert. But what had happened to them? What had interrupted them? Shen Ti, virtually helpless, would be placed in the boat first. Why hadn't the others followed? And who had cut the boat loose?

He looked at the girl. "You wouldn't care how many there was, would you? No, don't answer me. Keep your mouth shut."

He went to the stern, handed in the painter, coiled it. He unshipped the forward oars, seated himself, and began to row.

This was a big boat for one man to handle. On impulse Abner turned it and made for the land he'd just left. Holding the painter, he scrambled ashore, snatched up the pistol, thrust it behind his belt, and a moment later was off again. Shen Ti opened her eyes at that, but she said nothing.

Abner was in a hurry, but at the same time he did not wish to bump the bark. Stealth was called for.

Seated like this, his head now above the low-lying mist, he could see the shore, and whenever he turned his head he could see the ship they approached.

He made for the starboard side, where a Jacob's ladder hung from the waist. The other end of the painter, cut clean, was fastened to it. There was not a sound from the deck.

Abner made the boat fast. He cocked the pistol behind his belt, even though he might shoot off his own toes if he banged the striker against anything. He placed a firm forefinger over his mouth and scowled down at Shen Ti, who smiled again, languorously, and stretched her arms out towards him.

He unsheathed his cutlass. He needed both hands to climb, so he put the cutlass between his teeth. It made him feel like a story-book pirate, but he couldn't help that. There was nobody to see him anyway, except a slut from the slums of Singapore.

He climbed to the waist.

Chapter Twenty-Four

I<small>T IS</small> not natural for a person who seeks something to look upwards, unless he happens to be skipper of a sailing vessel. And then it is simply because he worries about his canvas. The scrutiny is instinctive, not reasoned. Should he crack on a little more, and if so where? Or—might it be better to do a bit of reefing? He can *hear* the wind, *smell* the weather, and even if he happens to be below he can *feel* the straining of timbers; but if he would learn about the set of his sails he must look aloft.

When Abner threw a leg over the gunnel his eyes, naturally, swept the deck. They came upon nothing unusual. Every line was coiled, the planks were clean, the buckets hung, the belaying pins neatly racked. But— there was nobody in sight.

The instant his foot touched the deck, however, his eyes were lifted. By the time his other foot had struck the deck he had his pistol out and was cocking it with his thumb.

One of the Lascars, barefooted, stood on the main boom, just forward of the mast itself, against which he balanced himself lightly with his left hand. In that position he was only about fifteen feet above the waist, and only a few feet above the level of the poop and forward decks. He faced aft. Had he turned to look he could easily have seen Abner approach in the longboat, but he was absorbed in the sight of something or somebody on the poop—somebody or something that Abner could not see.

Abner could see the poop only as far as the forward end of the skylight. He could see the top of the wheel, but not the binnacle. Most important of all, he could not see the transom, the cabin hatch.

This Lascar was a lithe little man named Sahrk, a troublemaker from the beginning. He had small, vulperine eyes, a mouth that was like a razor slash. In all his movements he was oblique; he sidled, never looked directly at anybody or anything. Yet he was a dangerous character. He had the agility and the balance of a cat, and he was venomous. Sahrk had been one of the two hands in the mainmast shrouds the second day out of Singapore when somebody had tried to brain Captain Smith with a belaying pin. Had he also been the man who threw the knife at Abner a few mornings after that? It seemed likely. That he was an expert knife-thrower was made evident now by the way he held, very lightly and by the blade, a long thin dagger. This was not a sheath knife, such as any sailor might be expected to carry; it was longer, more delicate and looked as if it had no edge, only a point, like a Scottish dirk. Abner watched him carefully.

The bark was utterly still, no hint of a motion. Time crawled, then seemed to have stopped altogether. The man on the boom, watchful like a panther, didn't stir. Abner, with raised right arm, felt as though he had stood for hours in that position.

Suddenly, and with the speed of a striking snake, the Lascar drew the knife back and raised it to throw.

In that instant Abner shot him.

The man did not at once fall to the deck. Slammed sideways, he sprawled along the boom. He lay neatly balanced for a moment, teetering. Then he slipped off. Had there been any roll of the bark he might have been pitched into the sea. As it was, he struck the gunnel. He seemed to grunt. Once again he sprawled full-length, with the movement of a man who flops upon a mattress. He was on his belly, the width of the waist away from Abner, and his chin was propped high, so that he stared right at his skipper. But though his eyes were open he wasn't seeing anything.

Abner raced for the poop ladder and scrambled up. He leaped over the top of the skylight, hearing the crack of a rifle as he did so, and seeing a strip of splinters spring from the deck.

Then he lay still, catching his breath behind the skylight, inches from the open cabin hatch. He heard Anne in that hatchway before he even turned his head. He actually heard her breathing, so still was the ship. And when he did turn it was with a smile. He reached over and kissed her. Then, peering around the edge of the skylight, he said, "Don't let the top of that rifle stick up. It warns them you're surfacing for a look."

"They can't see down into the hatch from up there."

"They could from the shrouds. One of 'em was on a boom a little while ago, all ready to sling steel into your neck. That didn't sound like a pistol. They got one of the Kentucky's?"

"Two of them. This is the third. But neither of the pistols. I still have them."

"Ball? Powder? Caps?"

"Some. Not much."

"Good." Still flat, still watching, he skidded his empty pistol to her. "Then reload this. The way I showed you with the rifles, only you don't put quite as much powder

L

in. And pass that Kentucky over here. Mind you hold it low now!"

The waist of the *Forest* was long but it was not deep. No door opened upon it. It could be reached only from the sea, as Abner had reached it, or else by one of the four ladders, two forward, two aft, all in plain sight and unprotected. True, it was cut by both main hatches, but these were well battened down, and it was impossible to believe that they could have been worked open from beneath, even supposing that the hands by superhuman efforts had succeeded in breaking from the forecastle into the forward hold. Nobody had been in the waist when Abner first saw it, after climbing up from the longboat, and the only person there when he'd quit it was not likely to take any further part in the fighting.

In other words, these two forces occupied almost identical forts, wooden forts separated only by this waist. Most of the stores were aft, but there was storm biscuit and water forward, enough at least for a siege of several days. The swivel gun was aft, but it could not be so manipulated as to swing the muzzle forward, this being the blocked-out part of its arc. It had been set that way lest by a slip it should be fired through the bark's own standing rigging. The poop controlled the helm, the forward deck the anchor; and at the moment neither was any good without the other. There were no portholes. The only way to leave or enter either fort was by means of a square, comparatively small hatch, a trapdoor flush with the deck, protected in neither case by any manner of shield. There was also, aft, the skylight; but this was a strong structure, if small, and for all practical immediate purposes immovable. Forward they had two Kentucky rifles and their knives;

aft were three pistols, two knives, one rifle, one cutlass.

The odds in manpower were overwhelming, but day was at hand and Ab had no intention of surrendering, upon any terms.

The Lascars could not gain anything by waiting. Certainly they could take over the vessel; yet they could not hope to pour out of the forecastle, tumble into the waist, cross it, climb to the after deck, and overcome Ab and Anne without losing at least two or three of their men. Abner did not believe that they would do that.

So he watched the forward deck. The hatch up there was open, and several times a head or a pair of hands showed momentarily, but Abner did not shoot. As a marksman he was no more than average, and he had no wish to advertise this fact.

"You might tell me about it," he said at last. "How'd they get those guns and the powder?"

"Shen Ti." Her voice was bitter as she rammed the wadding into the pistol. "She sneaked them forward. The ungrateful little bitch."

Her language hit him like a body punch, yet he chuckled inwardly.

"I'm sorry," Anne added, though she did not sound sorry. "But when I think of how I took care of her, and washed her——"

Abner shrugged. He might have pointed out that he had told her what kind of woman Shen Ti was. But he refrained. The truth is, Abner would have given up a dozen Chinese trulls, royal or otherwise, in order to have this one remaining source of friction between him and Anne removed.

"She sneaked out?"

"She did. She must have made two or three trips, quiet as a mouse, just before dawn."

A board, evidently ripped from one of the bunks, had been tossed out of the forecastle hatch. Now another one followed this, and another. Abner was watching them.

"She was going back. She was returning to her sin, the way the Bible tells us that a dog returns to its vomit."

She had finished loading the pistol, and to emphasize her point she all but slammed this down on the deck. "One of the tindals woke me up. I took the only rifle that was left and we went topside. They'd been putting things into the longboat."

"So I saw."

"And *she* was there, in the boat already. And since she was the one who'd caused all the trouble, I ordered them to cut her loose. Then, when they didn't move. I cut her loose myself."

"But if——"

"She couldn't have drifted out through the pass. I was sure of that. And if she drifted ashore—well, that's where she wanted to go anyway, wasn't it? Most likely I thought, she'll just go nowhere at all—I knew she wouldn't have sense enough to use the oars—until you came back, and then you could take care of her."

"Well, thank you."

"Because *I* wash my hands of her."

Two other boards had been poked gingerly out of the forecastle, and Abner tried to guess what it was they were attempting to do up there. Perhaps they meant to prop the boards in such a way as to form a sort of wooden wall or fence between the hatch and the larboard gunnel. Then they could slip behind that barrier, one by one, from out of the hatch, and mass there, crouching, and then suddenly topple the thing over and make a concerted rush. Abner thought they would hesitate a long time before actually risking this. However, if he did see any preparations for such a move, he would try to break them up with a few well-placed shots. At this distance his Kentucky rifle could pierce two inches of oak, and the bunk-boards out of which this fence was being built were second-grade pine.

"There were six or seven of the Lascars," Anne continued, "and more coming up every minute. The tindal didn't dare turn his back to them, so, as I said, when I couldn't get anybody to obey my order I took his knife and climbed down that ladder and cut the boat adrift myself. I hated to turn my own back on them, but I did it fast, before they had a chance to think."

He felt proud of her as he listened and kept watching the forecastle hatch.

The real reason for the fence, he had decided, was to protect men who might leap out of the hatch, cross the short distance behind it to the larboard gunnel, and slither over that gunnel. They would have to go over; the hawsehole on that side, as on the other, was too tiny for even the smallest of them. They could then drop into the sea, or, more likely, catch the anchor cable there and slide down. The mist was being burned off, and once in the water any one of the Lascars could swim ashore— any one, that is, who could swim. More likely, though, they meant to stay close to the vessel and work their way to the Jacob's ladder. Then they could either climb that ladder and so get into the waist unseen, and be in a good position for a telling rush—or else they could push off in the longboat, complete with trollop. He believed that they would do the latter. By staying directly forward of the bark they could remain out of his range for a long while.

The thing to do would be pot the first one as he tried to wriggle over the gunnel. The fence wasn't high enough. A certain amount of backside would inevitably be exposed —a far better target than any he had heretofore been offered; and it could only be offered in that one spot. Abner supposed that when the first man was ready to try the dash they would make some effort to divert his attention. He did not know what form this would take, but he braced his elbows, waiting.

"You should have got into the boat yourself," he said to Anne.

"And desert the ship?"

"Don't be so noble. They couldn't do anything with it anyway. Not a one of them can navigate."

"Mutineers have taken over ships they couldn't navigate before."

"Well, that's true. But they couldn't get this vessel outside anyway. She just won't fit. Draws too much water, even at high tide. We came through that pass with a push, in a freak storm. We'll never go back out through it—not loaded the way we are."

"What do you plan to do, then?"

He didn't answer, but asked her to go on with her story.

"I climbed up again. They were close to that poor tindal, ready to slash at him, and I handed him his knife back and took the rifle. The other tindal came out, but some of them grabbed him and pushed him back. I think he wanted to be loyal. He just didn't dare."

Abner nodded.

"That Tamil boy too. The one who waits on us. I think it was the same thing with him," she said. "Even after the tindal got his knife back they still kept after him. He was cut in three or four places. He sort of staggered. He must have been mighty weak. So I aimed the rifle at nearest man and closed my eyes and pulled the trigger. And nothing happened."

Abner nodded again. "Probably the cap. You can't rely on them."

"Right away I re-cocked it, and then they really drew back a bit. That gave the tindal and me a chance to get up here."

"He's below now?"

"Yes. In your cabin."

"Conscious?"

"Oh, yes. But he's weak. He needs bandaging. I didn't dare stay down there long, and when I came up they were edging over. I'd put another cap on by that time, and I pointed the rifle again and fired—and this time it went off. They all ran back to the forecastle, and I ducked down here. Then everything was still for a long time. Too still. I thought I'd better come up for another look. And then you came along, thank God."

"You did a good job," Abner muttered. "You did a lovely job."

"That's the first time I ever shot a rifle."

"I hope it'll be the last."

"I hope so too. Now if——"

A man had started to wriggle over the larboard gunnel. He moved fast, but Abner had been prepared for this. Abner even permitted the man to get halfway over, so that he presented the largest, most humped-up target. Then Abner fired.

There was a scream, followed by a loud splash.

"Look out," cried Anne. *"Here they come!"*

Chapter Twenty-Five

PROBABLY IT had not been planned. Probably it was a spur-of-the-moment business touched off by the sailors' taut nerves and the scream of the one who'd been wounded. They did not all come out of their cover; only four or five did so, but these included the two with the Kentucky rifles. They were yelling at the top of their lungs, dodging back and forth, running fast.

There were two ladders from the waist up to the after deck, one beside each gunnel, and from where he lay, flat on his belly beside the open hatch, Abner commanded the top of each. They were equidistant from him. Anne was half in and half out of the hatch, standing on the ladder that led to the cabin passageway.

"Get down," Ab shouted to her.

He held his fire, though this was hard to do. He might have potted one of those running riflemen at the far end of the waist—when they got farther aft, near the ladders, they would be out of his sight—but because of the distance and because of the way they were twisting and dodging he was afraid he'd miss. There might be no time to reload.

There was a cocked pistol on the deck beside his elbow. He planned to use this on the second man to appear—if he had a chance.

The first sailor came on the left, the larboard ladder, foolishly holding his rifle ahead of him. Abner saw the gun first and so was prepared for the man who followed it.

The man's face was all hatred, eyes aflame, mouth open in a savage yell. He did not wait to scramble off the ladder but fired as he came, holding the rifle full-length like a pistol. Smoke blanked him out, then instantly lifted, yellowish and thin. Abner felt something slap the top of his shoulder as though somebody had been congratulating him. It was odd: a sensation of camaraderie from a stroke that had been made in sheer malice. Ab knew he was wounded, but he had fired at the same time as the other.

The Lascar, likely enough, never knew what hit him. He seemed to spin backwards, like a bowling pin hit squarely by the ball. His rifle clattered to the poop, not falling, as he did, into the waist.

Ab dropped his own rifle and picked up the pistol. He was propped on one elbow, again prepared for a close-up shot, when the second man appeared at the starboard ladder. This man came very fast, rifle ready.

Nobody could have missed at that distance, but Abner had the advantage of position. Deliberately he lined up his sights on the space between the Lascar's eyes and pulled the trigger.

There was a sharp click, nothing more.

The Lascar grinned, realizing what had happened. His fright passed as he heard the sound of a defective percussion cap, and now he took his time as he levelled his gun.

There was an explosion that must have been inches from Abner's ear. Gunsmoke streaked past his face. The Lascar went over backwards like a well-oiled mechanical manikin, like one of those brightly painted wooden figures in a Bavarian clock. He simply wasn't there any more.

"Nice shooting," grunted Abner, and rose.

Crouching low, he recovered the first Lascar's rifle and passed it to Anne while she slid to him the other reloaded Kentucky. He knelt now at the head of the larboard ladder. From there he could command the whole waist.

It was empty of living men. But two Lascars were on the forward deck, both trying at once to get back into the forecastle hatch while a third was climbing the ladder to that deck, holding in one hand the rifle that had fallen into the waist with the man Anne had shot.

"Hold it," Abner shouted.

The man had reached the top of the ladder. He turned, went to one knee, and pointed the rifle.

Startled, Ab fired.

They must both have fired at the same instant, for though Abner did not hear the other shot a groove of splinters appeared in the deck next to his right foot and something went *plunk* into the taffrail behind him.

Where his own ball went he never knew. The Lascar, rifle and all, leaped nimbly into the forecastle hatch.

"First round," Ab muttered.

He turned back to thank Anne, who, to give herself something to do and hide her nervousness, was reloading the pistol she had fired. The hot barrel burned her. There was still a wisp of yellow-grey smoke at the muzzle.

"They may not try it again," Abner said. "Maybe that Tamil boy down there and the other tindal, they might talk 'em out of a second rush. Especially now that they've lost several leaders. But I guess we can't count on that."

He squatted by her side and reloaded the Kentucky rifle he had fired. Then he reloaded the one the Lascar had let fall, shaking his head meanwhile. "Pesky things. But they're certainly much better'n the old flint-and-steel."

He placed the weapons in convenient spots on the deck. He put a cutlass there too. He lit a cigar, using a match from his waterproof case, and began recalculating the odds.

Three of them, not two, held the after part of the ship. The tindal below, the one who'd been beaten, could be brought into action if needed. Moreover—and perhaps this was even more important—Anne had proved herself cool-headed in an emergency. She would not break down.

They had two of the three Kentucky rifles now, while the Lascars had but one. They still had two pistols, and plenty of ammunition. They had several cutlasses and knives. As far as Abner knew, there were no cutlasses in the forecastle, though of course there were knives.

In the waist were three dead or dying men, including Sahrk, the knife-thrower and apparent ringleader. It was reasonable to suppose that the other two, the ones who'd held the rifles in the attack on the poop, at least had been among the boldest of the crew. Another man, a fourth, had gone overboard, shot.

This would leave twelve men in the forecastle. Of these, the second tindal and the Tamil boy, Yok, almost certainly were being forced. Perhaps half of the remaining ten— this was only a guess—had no enthusiasm for the mutiny, only seeking to save their own skins.

So—the odds weren't as bad as they had been a short while before. But they were bad enough.

"Do you think they might break into that hold again and get some more opium and drive themselves into a frenzy?" Ann asked.

He shook an impatient head.

"You got the same idea about pipers that so many folks at home seem to have," he said. "The only time they get into any kind of frenzy is when they've been having as much of the stuff as they want and then suddenly they can't get it any longer. *That* drives 'em crazy. But as far as those hands up there getting hopped up right now is concerned, why, I'd like nothing better. Then we could just stroll up forward and take over as easy as you please. No—no such luck."

He had lighted the cigar for several reasons. It was a gesture that he hoped would reassure Anne Mackenzie. Not that she was very edgy—all considered, she was doing wonderfully—but every little bit of confidence might help. Second, a smoke would taste good. His clothes were wet and steamy, clinging to his body, giving him a chill. Third, it had occurred to him that a cigar would serve as an excellent linstock in case he had occasion to fire the swivel gun. This was assuming that the regular linstock, already laid out, was damp; and probably it was at this hour. The fuse might well be damp too. The lighted end of a cigar could be applied to it again and again until it was properly burning, whereas, with seconds counting, it might take a long time to get the linstock well aglow.

The gun already was loaded and laid, aimed in the right direction. Now Abner rose, partly in order to stretch his legs, partly to take a look at the rocky spit of land over there and see if Kok Soo and the men from the *Firefly* had come. He needed them, badly. Even if he and Anne, with the possible aid of the tindal below, could hold off the Lascars until dark (after which they might swim ashore) or even if they could bluff them into surrender, which was unlikely, Abner alone could never handle those men and make them drive the bark clear to the anchorage at Whampoa, the port of Canton. The veteran Kok Soo and the hands from the *Firefly,* but especially that driver, Austin, would be absolutely necessary.

They were not in sight. Nobody was in sight. The shore was as bleak and bare as it had been when first Abner and Anne had seen it that morning after the storm. The far-away surf mumbled, throwing itself high in impotent despair. The seagulls squawked.

Ab worked the tompion out of the muzzle of the gun.

There was a whiplike crack behind him, and a chunk of lead went *ting* against the gun barrel, to ricochet into the waters of the lagoon.

He cried, "Hey!" and ducked. He needn't have done so. He might have taken his time; for they would use two minutes in reloading that rifle. Was he getting jittery? He puffed at his cigar.

"I think maybe we'd better have that tindal up from the cabin," he said at last. "See if we can't use him to talk the others out of the forecastle."

The man's face was ghastly, cut in half a dozen places, blue with bruises, puffed. As Anne had said, he needed bandaging. Yet he was impassive, listening to Ab's orders with no more expression than he might have displayed while receiving any routine deck instruction. At the end he nodded. He lay on the deck near the starboard ladder,

Abner kneeling behind and above him, covering the fore-castle hatch with one of the rifles, and he hollered.

The words were unintelligible to Captain Smith, but he had no doubt that the tindal was following orders.

He shouted that they should come out. There would be no further killings if they came out, and the case would be referred to an international maritime court of enquiry at Canton. But they must come out of the forecastle right away, and with their hands held high.

The tindal ended his tirade. There was silence.

"Tell 'em," Ab said at last, "that reinforcements are expected soon, and then nobody's going to be given another chance. Tell 'em that if worst comes to worst, before I let a single one of them get away I'll set fire to the ship—as soon as it's dark—and swim for it. Tell 'em we can all swim, all of us back here."

"Me no swim," muttered the tindal.

"Well, tell 'em that anyway."

The message was shouted; and for a long time afterwards it appeared that there would be no sort of response.

The answer, when it did come, came in unexpected form. There was a high shriek, a womanish sound—for one startled instant Abner even supposed that Shen Ti had somehow got from the longboat to the forecastle, from whence that sound came—and then the Tamil cabin boy, the captain's striker, Yok, burst forth.

He was in terror. A small man—not properly a "boy" at all—he was at odds with most of the Lascars and devoted to Captain Smith. Now he was screeching as he scrambled out of the hatchway.

"No burnee, cap'n! No burnee me!"

He leaped into the waist and started to run aft. A Lascar

appeared in the forecastle hatch, the remaining Kentucky in his hands.

"I come you! No burn——"

The Lascar fired, and Abner fired at the same moment.

Yok whirled completely around and dropped to his knees, sobbing in pain, his left hand cupped over the top of his right shoulder. Blood began to show between the fingers of that hand.

The Lascar let go of the Kentucky. He did not otherwise move. He could not have been badly wounded, and perhaps he had not been hit at all—perhaps he had dropped the rifle out of sheer fright. Now, cursing, he realized what he had done. He stooped to pick the gun up.

Abner seized the second rifle and shot him in the abdomen. The Lascar collapsed on deck, right on top of the Kentucky rifle.

"Yok!" Abner rose from one knee, snatching pistol and cutlass, leaving the rifles for Anne to reload. "Catchum-up gun-gun! Bringum here quick! Bringum gun-gun cap'n!"

The cabin boy, though still sobbing, acted fast. While blood gushed from the flesh wound on his shoulder he climbed to the forward deck and started to work the rifle from under the prone Lascar. Once those on the poop had that rifle the fight would be over.

Yok tugged hard. The rifle came free. Then a figure loomed in the hatchway, another Lascar, who either knew or guessed what was happening. He made a lunge for Yok, and Abner shot him dead.

Considering the fact that he was firing a pistol, a weapon hardly meant to carry that distance with any accuracy, it was crack marksmanship. Or maybe it was luck. Whatever the explanation, it ended the fight.

"Now that's enough," Abner roared. "Come out, every one of you!"

They might not know the words but they knew the tone of voice. And they remembered what the tindal had told them. The other tindal was the first to appear. Then one by one, holding their hands high, they came blinking and stumbling up onto the deck.

Abner counted them as they came. He had just checked the last one, and had nodded in grim satisfaction, when there was a volley of shots on the shore.

Ab spun on his heel. He had seen that each tindal now held a rifle while Anne held the third one, and Yok had a loaded pistol.

"Hold 'em there a minute," he commanded.

He ran to the swivel gun.

Chapter Twenty-Six

THE PLAN was not working out as it should. True, Kok Soo and the seven men from the *Firefly*, muskets in their hands, were retreating backwards towards the tip of the spit, and they were being pursued. But the pursuit was brisk, which Abner had not expected, especially since the pursuers had presumably been picked by Shap'ngtzai in person.

Then he saw the explanation. The Lord of Namoo himself, his attendants around him, a red umbrella held over his head, was being carried into battle. It was the mandarin's presence that had inspired his men, or frightened them, so that they kept close behind the fugitives, spread out in a thin, wavering line, kneeling now and then to aim. Their guns, smooth-bore muskets that made a hollow booming sound, would not carry far.

There were more of these pursuers than Ab had anticipated. Had Shap'ngtzai been relieved of his command, so that he couldn't pick the squad? It could be, of course, that the captain of the guard had seized this opportunity to get rid of his hated master by permitting him to walk straight into a trap, after which Shap'ngtzai might plan to turn upon those who had set that trap, killing two birds with one stone. Ab could only hope that this wasn't so. He had to trust the bald-headed warrior, who was supposed to hide himself and his own loyal followers in the small Stonehenge where Abner had tussled with Austin, and out of which Kok Soo had come. Shap'ngtzai was scheduled to come from that shelter at the right moment and fall upon the mandarin's men, finishing them. Was he in fact there, ready to strike? Or had palace politics eliminated him?

Kok Soo and the *Firefly* men now appeared to break ranks, as though in panic. Instead of an orderly retreat, facing the enemy, walking backwards, they turned and ran for the tip of the spit. This was in accord with their orders.

The mandarin's men, after a moment of apparent doubt, started to run after them.

Abner cut the fuse of the swivel gun off short, and

M

applied the lighted end of his cigar to it, blowing. It started to splutter. He sprang back.

The gun went off almost instantly, making a great roar. If anything was needed to complete the defeat of the Lascar crew—though such was not its purpose—this shot was it. They burst into a wail of fear, and some of them even threw themselves face down on the deck, pleading for mercy, believing as they did that they were about to be systematically slaughtered.

Its effect upon the mandarin's men was less definite. A few fell, many paused, as though puzzled, but others did not appear to have heard the shot, and these last kept doggedly on the trail of the fugitives, firing as they went.

Abner reloaded the swivel gun, inserted another fuse, touched it off again.

This time it was better. The pursuit ground to a halt. A few of the mandarin's men actually started to fall back, and the litter itself, red umbrella and all, was turned completely around and began to lurch and sway away from the stony spit—and towards the upthrust monolithic boulders.

But now Austin and those under him lost patience. They were supposed to drive the mandarin's men back, to keep after them, peppering them with occasional gunfire, but not mixing in their midst lest they spoil the target. They did not do this, perhaps because with their cut bare feet they were eager to get this business over with and believed that they could carry it off with one big rush.

They did not stalk the mandarin's men. They charged them.

This meant that Abner, though he had the swivel gun all loaded and laid, did not dare risk a third shot.

He climbed down into the waist and addressed the tindals.

"Keep 'em busy! Don't give 'em a chance to catch their breath! Make 'em work, work, work!"

Abner pointed to the cargo hatches to make clear what sort of work he meant.

"Open them, both of them! And then haul every single chest of that stuff up here on deck! All right—start now!"

He took Anne by the arm.

"Come on—we're going ashore. I won't leave you here again."

"With that—that *thing*?"

"Stop being so fussy! Come on!"

He seated her in the sternsheets but he himself went to the bow. He had told two Lascars to handle the oars. They made good speed to the spit.

Now the battle was not going well. The mandarin's men had rallied and they were moving towards the tip of the spit again—pushing Austin's small force before them.

"Don't wait for me," Abner shouted as he jumped ashore. "If they kill us, row for it."

Thus he joined the fight.

Austin, who had been trying to make his men stand, saw Ab, came up alongside him, and then the two advanced upon the mandarin's men, shaming the others into following suit.

In a moment they broke into a trot. Now muskets were banging before them, sounding like so many slammed doors. Great blobs of grey smoke appeared here and there, to waver a moment, then break into stringy streamers, and fade. The air was filled with the whine of bullets.

Abner paused only once, and then but briefly. Within a few yards of the kneeling Chinese he stopped long enough to aim and fire the pistol he held. It would be his only shot, and he wanted to make it count. It did. A musketeer doubled up, jerking spasmodically.

Then Abner tossed the pistol aside, shifted the cutlass to his right hand, and charged.

He had never cared particularly for fighting, and unlike so many men had never troubled to pretend that he did. But when he had to fight, he did it without slapping himself on the chest or waving his weapons. He was cold about the business, but he was thorough.

For several minutes he simply struck at everything in sight. The muzzle of a musket was thrust into his face and the trigger was snapped; but the gun didn't go off and Ab knocked it aside and kept swinging.

His left shoulder hurt him badly. He was no longer able to ignore it. Pain seared the whole length of his body. He was afraid he might faint.

Suddenly his ankle was grabbed from behind, and he went sprawling. The cutlass was wrenched from his hand. Three Chinese sprang at him with uplifted clubs. Abner was rolling as he struck the ground, and he must have rolled twelve or fourteen feet before he rose to his knees. He found a musket somebody had thrown away. He held it by the barrel and got to his feet. He was swinging the musket savagely when the mandarin's men broke.

Abruptly, where there had been furious fighters there were now only the backs of men who ran away.

What had happened? Swaying, blinking, panting, his shoulder on fire, Ab Smith surveyed the field.

Out of the forest of rocks other Chinese soldiers had appeared, and with yells of rage were falling upon the fugitives.

Abner and his men came to a stop, wiping the sweat off their faces. Their part in the fight was over. What remained would be no more than butchery, and there was no need for them to join in that. Shap'ngtzai had kept his end of the bargain. He would know what to do.

Ab hurried back to the tip of the spit, standing in front of Anne so that she could not see the messy work in progress. However, there was no drowning out the screams. Not much mercy was shown that morning on the island of Namoo.

Abner put the others, except Kok Soo, aboard the longboat, explaining that Austin was in command. Orders were to work the hands relentlessly, work them until they dropped from exhaustion. And their job was to dump the cargo into the lagoon.

"Abner! You can't do that," said Anne.

"I happen to be captain of this ship."

"But—that opium's worth almost a hundred thousand pounds!"

"You told me once you wished you could watch it all pitched into the sea. Well, now you have your wish."

"*Abner*, you must have a reason!"

"I have. But I haven't got time to give it to you now."

She started to get out of the boat.

"I'll stay with you."

"No, you won't. But *you* will," he said to Shen Ti, and crooked a finger at her. "Come here."

Twenty minutes later, halfway down the spit, he met Shap'ngtzai. The pirate chief, a monarch in his own right now, no longer a mere lieutenant to one of the Emperor's satraps, was very happy. He embraced his white friend and called for a feast. Abner shook an impatient head. He aimed to get out of there, not to stay around eating and drinking.

"Tell him I want my own squeeze," he said to Kok Soo. "The one we agreed on. Where is it?"

When this had been interpreted, Shap'ngtzai beamed. He led Abner to the litter and reached into it. Not casually, for he knew well the value of the thing, not contemptuously, but as easily as though handling, say, some ceremonial cape, he drew forth and dropped at Abner Smith's feet the body of the late Lord of Namoo, mandarin third class.

The thing on the ground looked like a broken mechanical toy, a doll that some child had mauled. There was no blood on it that Abner could see, though there was mud and there was plenty of spittle. The silken tunic was torn, the gold cloth unravelled. The cap with the symbolic blue button was gone, and the hair was seen to be thin, a muddy grey, wan, greasy. The fingernails, upon which so many years of careful tending had been spent, were muddied and smashed, cracked in places, as though the poor, nasty-minded little old man had struggled to save his own life.

No umbrella was held over this petty princeling now.

Worst of all was the head. It was this that gave the body its broken-doll appearance. The head was tilted back at an impossible angle, so that it pressed against the spine. The Lord of Namoo's neck had been broken—and broken by something of terrific power and strength. Already flies were beginning to gather.

"He say killem—killem hands—he say his own hands."

"I can well believe it," Abner muttered.

So Ralph Palmer had been avenged, as stipulated in the unwritten contract between these two. "'Vengeance is mine,' saith the Lord." And, all things considered, maybe it would have been better to leave it with Him.

Abner whistled for Shen Ti, who came to his side, looking up eagerly, expectantly.

He gave her a brusque push towards Shap'ngtzai.

"Well, here you are. And I only hope she turns out to be a humdinger. Now I must get back to my ship."

He lurched a little as he made his way to the end of the spit and to the boat that was waiting there. He was so tired that he had to be helped aboard the boat. All the while he could see the Lascars hauling those fine big chests of Malwa to the deck of the *Forest of Arden* and one by one pitching them into the sea.

He sighed. He certainly wasn't happy, and he was even a bit sick after what he had seen. But he was satisfied. It had been a good bargain.

Chapter Twenty-Seven

THE SUN shone bright on everything. On churches and monasteries, cream, oyster, milk-white, yellow; on incredible little sixteenth-century Iberian rococo houses, peeping out from the profusion of foliage strewn over the steep hillside; on ornamental brass cannons (they had been practicable once) mounted in the forts that seemed to beam benevolently rather than frown down upon the quaint, improbable little city of Macao.

The sun shone on the crescent of the Praya Grande with its water-steps and jetties, its broad promenade where the Chinese scuffed and scuttled along, their hands hidden in their sleeves, where the Portuguese sedately paced, clad in gleaming white, while bland, impenetrable Englishmen, generously but neatly bewhiskered, stood in solemn groups, discussing, not, as you might have supposed, the nebular hypothesis, Platonism, or the future of mankind, but—how to make more money.

The sun shone and glittered that afternoon on the wide blue entrance of Canton Bay, stippled, as always, with poly-chromatic craft; sampans that rode high; lorchas with slatted brown lateen sails; junks with monstrous big eyes painted on their bows; lean, low " centipedes " or " scram-bling dragons ", the multi-oared, extraordinarily fast ship-to-shore smuggling boats that operated by day as well as by night; and the local taxis too, maritime taxis, the " egg-shells ", small, almost square, with high, arched, matted awnings, each of them propelled by a Chinese girl in blue trousers and smock, her black plaited hair tied with red cotton ribbons and stuck with artificial flowers, who as she drifted, alert for customers, sang an unintelligible but no doubt bawdy ballad.

The shipping was all Oriental. No European or American vessels were in sight. There were not many of them in port at this season; and such as there were, including the bark *Forest of Arden*, 350 tons, out of Stonington, Conn., U.S.A., were either up at the Whampoa anchorage, or else clustered off the Bogue, near the mouth of the Pearl River, or they were doing business with the floating godowns in the middle of the bay. In any event, they were not to be seen from Macao.

The sun shone too upon Captain Abner Smith. He grunted; he stretched. He would have liked a cigar, but propriety was all-important when you were far away from home, and you should never smoke while you're riding in a carriage with your wife. So he sighed, and tried to forget it.

"Missy she allee-samee come out soon," he assured the coachman.

She did. In yellow organdie trimmed with lilac velvet bows, she had a light step, and her brown satin shoes, with low heels, clicked joyously on the steps as she descended. Abner watched her in sombre pride. How some women did it beat all. Though there wasn't a shop in town you'd care to go into without a clothes-peg on your nose, here again was his wife, his bride of six weeks, looking like a lady straight from Paris.

The skirt was very wide, as it was short, following the fashion. The sleeves were enormously puffed, each held out by some sort of wire contraption you couldn't see. She wore a wide Leghorn hat trimmed with more flowers than you could shake a stick at; but just to make absolutely certain that no sun reached her face she carried over her left shoulder, with careful carelessness, a long-handled brown silk parasol fringed with lace. He offered her his arm.

"Captain," she said, "we should leave this place soon if we're to get to the Straits before the southwest monsoon sets in."

"Ma'am," he answered, "we should."

They had given up calling one another by their first names now that they were no longer sweethearts but married. Besides, they weren't on a small ship any longer. It was all a part of the formality of the East, where you were like an actor on a stage, with so many people watching you. For instance, as he handed her into the carriage she was smiling radiantly, while he appeared excessively grave, though in fact their respective feelings were the other way 'round.

"You made good terms for those nankeens and that patchouli," she conceded, "and there isn't a better time of the year to buy tea. *If* we only happened to be able to pay for it. They want cash and nothing but cash out this way."

"I know."

"And if you had not put all your trust in a notorious pirate——"

"Ma'am, we've had this out before."

"Nothing but cash," she repeated. "Oh, Abner," she cried suddenly, "I want to get back home!"

"Why, so do I," he confessed, turning to her.

But she hardened. "There's a fortune in it if you could

fill up with tea at that price. It's real Lapsang Souchong, too. I—I tried to raise some money on my uncle's name the other day——"

"I was afraid you had."

"—but they wouldn't do it. Why, they treated me like a Yankee. Money to buy clothes with, or for passage home, yes. But no real money."

"Shap'ngtzai——"

"You and your friend Shap'ngtzai! Sometimes I just don't understand you, captain. One day you haggle over a penny, and the next you throw thousands of pounds worth of merchandise to the bottom of the South China Sea."

"Not the bottom of the sea," he said. "Only to the bottom of that lagoon, which wasn't very deep where we were. And every single chest was originally caked in paraffin to make it waterproof in case we shipped any seas on the voyage."

"I know, I know! You've told me all that! And about how you saved time and maybe trouble by lightening the vessel and clearing out right away instead of waiting around for weeks while they brought up rafts. And now Shap'ngtzai will be able to fetch the stuff up as good as new. I understand all that. But—why didn't you demand silver in advance?"

"Because he didn't have it."

"The mandarin——"

"The mandarin never had it himself. He only made out that he had. What he planned to do was get a chest or two of the Malwa ashore and then arrest us and seize the ship, cargo and all, on a smuggling charge. What would happen to it after that—and to us—is anybody's guess."

"And so what you did, you made a deal with the Devil——"

"At least he admitted he was the Devil. He went under his right name."

"—and you expect him to live up to his end of the bargain? Captain, sometimes I think you are soft-minded."

"It ain't exactly what you'd do at home," he agreed, "but a heap of things are different out here."

"You'll get sacked, for sure. My uncle can get you another command, or at least a good mateship, but I'm going to have a hard time recommending you, captain. I was making notes to-day on what will eventually be my report to Sir Gordon, and I couldn't help thinking——"

"Before you go too far," offered Abner, "suppose we stop here."

It was a godown, or warehouse, facing the bay, a fairly new building, and, as godowns in Macao went, reputable and even clean.

"Why should we stop here?" Anne asked.

Somebody else had stopped before them. A hired carriage faced them, and in it was somebody very small and gorgeous, somebody whose face could not be seen because of the guards and the unceasing line of coolies between the two carriages. But whoever it was, it was a personage, for a ceremonial umbrella was held over the tiny person's head by a Chinese boy who squatted behind.

"To renew certain acquaintanceships," Abner answered formally as he handed his wife down.

The boxes the coolies toted from a barge into the godown were of a uniform size and shape, and obviously heavy. When jogged, they clinked; and since the Chinese, curiously enough, had no use for gold, it must have been silver. Some big payment for something. On and on the coolies trudged . . . crate after crate. . . .

The presence of so many godown guards, presumably a precaution against raids, might have seemed curious to a foreigner if it had been pointed out to him that the bald giant in slashed velvet and gold galon, who supervised the job, was a practising pirate, already one of the greatest thieves in that nest of thieves, the South China Sea.

The giant greeted them with a grin, which, however, he instantly erased, remembering his manners. He was a stunning figure. When he moved he scintillated.

Abner shook Shap'ngtzai's hand. Anne swallowed, and simply said, " How d'ye do? "

" He say," began an interpreter, " he bling whole plice."

" Tell him we knew he would," Abner said. " Tell him," he added, " we would like to be presented to his wife."

Anne whispered, " Captain, *no* ! "

Abner whispered, " Ma'am, *yes* ! And what's more, you're going to ask them both to dinner."

" Abner——"

" You're Gordon Mackenzie's niece, aren't you, and my wife? "

Shen Ti had never looked more doll-like. She didn't gloat, didn't even smile. She was so stiff in brocades and Shantung silk, so lavishly studded with zircons from Ceylon, chrysoberl, quartz, peridote from the island of Zebirget, and nephrite and jadeite and chloromelanite and pearls, that it could be she did not dare to stir. She knew never a word of what the self-possessed white female said to her, but this didn't matter, for a boy would be sent with a written invitation soon—as soon as the deal for the tea had been closed.

The whole scene went off very well indeed.

"It's all there, down to the last dollar," Abner reported when they were in the carriage again. "We saved a heap this way. The only thing we had to pay was the squeeze, and we're well rid of her. On the other hand, *she* was never so happy before in her life. You mustn't worry about her immortal soul, my dear. Things are—well, they're sort of different out here in the East. Only reason they were late is because I'd stipulated bar silver instead of sycee. You yourself suggested that, remember?"

She threw her arms around him, to the amazement of the persons along the Praya Grande.

"Abner, I love you!"

"There, there," he said, embarrassed, yet grinning; and he reached over her shoulder as he hugged her, and gave her backside a loving little slap. "There, now!"

She straightened, holding her chin up, retrieving the smile, while Abner, for the benefit of passers-by, renewed his expression of solemn sobriety.

"One thing I will say, captain, and that is that, while we were lucky this time, I most certainly am going to advise my uncle not to invest in opium smuggling. Don't you agree with me?"

"There's better ways to make a living," said Abner. "Easier ones, anyway."

To the Reader

If you would like to be advised of our new books as and when published, please send us a card giving your name and address, and this will ensure that you receive these particulars regularly

---

ROBERT HALE LIMITED
63 Old Brompton Road London S.W.7